GEORGINA CAMPBELL

MEMOIRS

Cirencester

Published by Memoirs

MEMOIRS
PUBLISHING

25 Market Place, Cirencester, Gloucestershire, GL7 2NX
info@memoirsbooks.co.uk www.memoirspublishing.com

First published in England, August 2012

Book jacket design Ray Lipscombe

ISBN 978-1909304185

Printed in England

When we were little

Time ago little piece still there was a group of friends, Leona, Shelly, Maggie, Sonia and me, Jennie. We were all good girls and had big plans for ourselves. This is how it all began.

The first memory I have was when we were five and it was my birthday. My mum had invited some kids to come over - it was going to be brilliant. Mum was sorting out the sandwiches, cakes, sweets and juice. The table was so pretty, mum had bought me a new dress and shoes and I felt like a princess jumping around like the kid I was. We had games, music and pass the parcel. Mum even put my hair in ringlets, I loved it so much.

The doorbell rang and I ran to answer it. I could hear Mum from the kitchen say 'walk, don't run!' With that I tripped and cracked opened my head. Party, wot party? I spent the rest of the day at the hospital, and seven stitches and one lolly later I was allowed to go home. Dress ruined, head shaved, what a birthday I had.

The years seemed to fly by. Now we were teenagers talking about where we would be ten years from now. Shelly's the mum if you know what I mean, she's only 14 but she has this motherly thing about her, she wants to be a doctor, very caring. She's got dark hair, pretty girl always wanting to help. I remember when we were about nine and we found a hurt bird. I couldn't even look at it, Maggie was shouting 'It's got germs leave it, don't touch it!' It was so funny, but Shelly took off her jumper and put it around this little thing and took it home. I thought she would have given up on it, but she didn't. Her mum wasn't too pleased, but what could she say?

Maggie's nearly 15. She's very serious, always reading, big books not comics, nothing like that. Real life crimes, you know, deep shit, really dark. Sometimes she's cool, but then other days she ain't easy. Like when Leona had her first-ever kiss with a boy named Mark, all hell broke loose, I'm telling you when Maggie found out she went nuts. She hit the boy so hard there was blood all over the place, we never saw him again, no joke.

Leona's a nice girl, but too easy going, trusting anything anyone tells her, I've heard her mum go off on one.

'See you, yer? You best fix up and don't watch the things people tell you, like when your little friend was chatting a whole heap of rubbish, what's her name?'

'Sonia, mum.'

'Watch her, that's right, lord help us.' Leona's mum is a bit nuts. She cracks me up, she preaches all day long.

Going back to Sonia, she is very straight. Everything must be done just so and she don't ever get involved in nothing. Her dad is a policeman. We don't really go there much, if you know what I'm saying.

And now a little about me. My mum's English and my dad's Jamaican. I am one of five girls, slap bang in the middle, number three. No brother to look after us, so if something happened we would have to stand and fight. Yep, that's right, I'm the rebel, the black sheep of the family.

We got good parents, they done what they could, both hard working but it just wasn't enough. Mum would try and make ends meet. There was no money for nothing, times were hard. They worked all hours.

The things we do

That's when it began. I started staying out late, meeting new people, getting mixed up in all kinds of things, just having a laugh really. Claire's one of the girls I met up west. She's cool and her brother's hot. He's got a girl. I don't like her, she's two-faced. I remember her. I'll have to watch that one still.

Getting ready to go out, gonna meet Claire, pick up a little green!

Phone rings, it's Claire.

'Wot's up, where are you?'

'At Naz's picking up, I soon reach u, kool.'

Maggie was there smoking!

'Wot's up G? she said, arms out, 'Haven't seen you for time, wot's good?'

'I'm off out tonight, party, come man!'

I said to her holding her tight, 'She's my girl. We have to catch up get some joke'. So with that we leave. It's a 10-minute walk.

So we get to Claire's, have a drink and roll a spliff, put on two tunes and catch some joke, dancing round like fools all of us. Then Kriss comes in with his boys Jay and Phil. I didn't even know where to put my face, I'm like a kid when he's around. Kriss is Claire's brother, he's so... what can I say? He's my mates brother, can't go there even though I want to.

Jay's kool, he's what u call a sweet boy, pretty, well dressed, nice.

I've only met Phil a few times, he's a giggle.

'So we're all reaching this thing then?' Kriss said.

I looked at Maggie like oh shit, thinking what, all together?

'Where's Kelly at?' I said. That's his girl. No one answered me but I can feel a vibe in the room, so I say no more about it.

So by now everyone's a bit mash up, feeling nice, the boys are showin us their moves and their pulling power. They ain't gettin no gal like that, we were laughin so hard. The cabs are here, someone shouted.

As Claire was falling into the car she was telling Kriss to lock the front door.

'It's done, shut her up, she's lean up an we ain't even reach yet' he said.

The cab we were in stunk, the smell was nasty. I said to the driver 'Can I smoke?' and he nodded.

'Can you change the music bruv?' I said and he put on the radio, some soft soul, that was all right but the smell, even my smoke, weren't helping.

We pulled up and got out of the car the music was banging, people everywhere. Then I caught myself looking at Kriss in a way I shouldn't.

'Claire's so drunk, how much has she had?' he said, I don't know.

We know who lives in the house so we took Claire upstairs and put her on the bed. My heart starts racing, I don't know what's going on, Kriss holds my hand and draws me into him. I don't know where to look, I've liked him for a while now. Shit he's kissing me. I pull away.

'What about Kelly?'

'Wot bout her, come ere.'

'Na, I don't wanna get hurt and catch-up in a madness and Claire...'

'What bout Claire, she knows I like u for time.'

'So why Kelly?'

'It just went that way but that's gone now, come.'

'Na I can't, I have to go' I say but all the time that's where I want to be.

4

'Wot swear down you just gonna leave like that, cool!' I could see he was a bit pissed off.

'I can't do this right now Kriss? Make sure Claire gets home OK.'

I had to get out of there, I could feel myself slipping. I went to find Maggie, where is she I can't see her, then I hear her chatting up one guy. She's got no taste, there ain't even a word for it. Yes there is, ruff.

'Mags I'm making a move, what you doing with that?' sometimes my mouth gets me into trouble!

'Nothing babe' she said, grinning like the cat that got the cream.

'I've got to go, what you doing?'

'Staying' she said, 'why you going?'

I gave her a hug and kiss.

'I just need to leave, I'm kool though, Claire's upstairs watch her yer, love you babe, bell you later.'

I started walking to get the bus home and then heard my name being called. I turn around and it's Kriss. I stopped and waited for him to catch up, I was so nervous my heart was pumpin. He wasn't havin any of it. He's putting his arm round me and trying to kiss my neck.

'Wot's wrong with you?' I said.

'I can't help myself, you know how I feel about you.' I didn't say anything to him, I just kept walking. He was a bit drunk, nice with it but drunk. I stopped and looked at him. I couldn't help myself, before I know it I was kissing him. It was all I thought it would be, I couldn't stop myself. I can't even explain how he made me feel. I know it sounds a bit weird but I just wanted the bus to come so I could stop the madness.

I woke up the next morning thinking I dreamt it all, that made me feel better, then my doorbell went. I opened it.

'Kriss, what you doing here this early?'

'I need to talk.'

'OK' I said and let him in. We went to the kitchen to make tea. I know he's been home cos he's changed his clothes, so what's he doing here? Tea's on the table.

'So what's up?' I say to him.

'Boy' he says 'I need to know how u feels about me. Can anything happen?'

I so want to say yes, but I say 'what are we doing, no way!'

'So what was last night about?'

'I was mash up, it didn't mean anything.'

He looked at me with hurt in his eyes. I wish I hadn't said that now cos I didn't mean it. I've liked him for so long and I'm throwing it away before it's had the chance to grow into something.

'OK the truth is I've liked you as long as I can remember, but we can't do nuffin about it. We're friends and it should stay that way.'

With that he got up and walked over to where I was sittin and pulled me up to him.

'I'm not letting this go, u know that don't you?' He's kissing me on the lips and I can feel myself gettin hot. He gives me a hug, then goes. I watch him out the window thinking what the fuck was that about? I'm smiling to myself, but in the real world it wouldn't work, he's a street man wrapped up in a hole heap of things.

Then my dad walks in. 'Morning Jennie.'

'Ello luv' I reply, kissing him.

'Wanna cuppa?'

'Mmmm that would be nice, where's mum?' he asked,

'Not home yet' I say, walking to put the kettle on.

'All right I'm gonna take my tea with me, nite.'

Dad drives a black cab, days are nights and nights are days if you know what I mean.

Had a nice bath, got dressed, made a phone call, was out the door, gonna link up with Maggie, I never got to see her much last nite. Wanna see wot happened with that ting she pulled. Don't know what she's thinking.

Down the café meeting the girls

I walked in and Maggie is with Shelly, she's been away, I haven't seen her for time. 'Wot's good girlies?'

'Come ere!' Shelly grabs at me, 'Where you been hun, what you been up to?' She hands me some photos. 'Who's this geezer?'

'Hold on a minute.' He's in all of them. 'Wot's going on, is there something you wanna tell us babe?'

'That's Jason, we spent a lot of time together, he's well nice, you're gonna meet him soon he's coming over' she said like nuffin

'Coming over an staying where, with who don't get me mad' Maggie blows face vex!

'Fix up Maggie don't handle her like that, but for true where's he staying.' I ask her,

'At mine most probably if it's kool with my mum, you will see for yourself anyway.'

'So wot we doing for the rest of the day' I say

'Let's go up west' Shelly says.

I'm not feeling that! 'Mags wot u sayin?'

'Let's go to mine, my dad's away, let's go.'

We get to Maggie's, her mum don't live there any more, she's got a young ting, he's kool but Mags can't stand him. Well he's with her mum, init.

'So wot happened last Jen, how you jus duck out like that?'

'It's nuffin man, leave it.'

'Don't try swing things round, wot was you doin fam? You forget i was there, I see you.

'So....nuffin, jus' chillin. I left with them lot anyway, Maggie was watchin me a bit funny, then said Kriss didn't come back with us.'

'Wot?' I said.

'Wot do you mean wot?' kissing her teeth. I'm gonna knock her out; I don't know how I kept my hand off her!

'You know something. I don't business where Kriss was or wasn't, it's nothing to do with me.'

That hit me hard! I feel hurt.

'Wot you acting like that for'

This girl doesn't know when to shut up star!

'Shut up, ur pissing me off, why you always got something to say?'

'Wot you talking about Jen?'

'Just shut up Maggie, you make me sick sometimes, wot's wrong with you?'

'Sorry babe' she said like nuffin, they say the truth hurts an yer, it's a punch in the face cuts an all!

But I can see she ain't, she ah fucking bitch anyone with eyes can see how much I check for him!

All Maggie does all day every day is drink and smoke weed, I mean not putting her down or anything like that cos I love her, she's been though a lot in her life, things will never be the same after what happened, her uncle abused her when she was six, that's why she's so fucked up. And to make matters worse her dad did five years for chopping him up, I'm talking about her mum's brother you know. Deep shit, her dad was in jail, her mum's a drunk and she was only six. I mean we were young but I remember hearing my parents talking about it, that's when everything changed.

I saw her at school but that was about it, I used to ask her to tea but she never came. It wasn't until we started secondary school we really got to know what happened to her and how it damaged her. We grew together but she loves catch up in people's business, that's why I stay away.

I smoke but I'm doing what I need to do. I'm in college training to become a chef, it's hard work.

At home mum's cooking dinner, everyone's in, that makes a change, well I say everyone, my older sisters Marie and Anne don't live at home any more, they're both married with kids. The two younger ones Abbie and Lucie are seven. And trust me they're a hand full at the best of times.

We sat down to eat, I weren't feeling it though.

'You not hungry Jennie' mum said.

'Na I'll have it later' and went to my room,

Got a text off Claire, wanting me to go over to hers.

Sent one back, *not feeling too well x* and left it at that. A few days went by, been going college making bread and cakes. Wicked, so many different types of dough, understanding what goes in what, and how it all works. I love my course. Claire's been dinging off my phone; I will have to go check her, put on a brave face.

Can't do this any more

Gonna get something to eat, then I will pass round. I'm hoping Kriss ain't there. As I reach Claire's who pulls up, Kelly looking for Kriss. I say 'Claire can we get out of here, don't really wanna hear this.'

'Why wot's happened is something wrong, is that why I ain't seen you fam, are you OK?'

'I'm kool, just one of them days init.' I wonder what's going on back there.

'Sorry babe I need to go sort something out, I'll bell you.'

'Jen wot's wrong, talk to me hun.'

'Nothing' I say, she can see I'm not myself. I feel like a fuckin idiot, is he playin me?

At home doin my course work, my phone rings, it's Kriss I'm not answering it, by now 10 missed calls.

The door goes!

'What do you want Kriss?' in a way I'm glad, it shows me he cares.

'Can you just hear me out please?' he sounds down. Don't really wanna hear whatever it is.

'Please babe?'

I let him in.

'So can we talk on the level' he said.

'Why Kriss, you made me feel like a fool?'

'Na man I never told her to come, I don't want that, I told her, come on I'm here to sort this fucking shit out, na na sorry! Sort things out with you, she's an all right kinda girl but I don't want that, she knows how I feel about you.'

'What do you mean?' I said, that was nice to hear though.

'I told her it's you not her that I want, believe me.'

'We can't.' I've been fighting this for so long now I just don't know. He says, 'Can't wot?'

'Be together, you're on road.' He don't see it!

'I don't wanna get caught up in all of that.'

He hugged me kissing the side of my face. 'You won't get involved in nuffin, so what you thinking Jen?'

'I don't know, I need time?'

'Babe I'm going give you some space, come find me when you're ready.' Squeezing me tight, he smells so nice. Kissing me softly on the lips.

'You gonna walk me to the door babe?' he says, taking me by the hand.

I really like him, At the door he turns, leans towards me, we kiss. I can feel my heart beating like it's gonna break though my chest, I've never felt like this about anyone, I mean no one ever. He pulls away and says 'Babe gonna see you soon'.

I watch him drive away; I put the radio on. Must have fell asleep, cos the next thing I heard was mum saying 'Jen I've made you a cuppa'. Then it's 'is everything all right darling?'

'Yer mum, it's college. I'm just tired, going to bed. love you. 'Night babe.'

I wake up to the twins jumping all over the place. No college off for two weeks it's end of term, that means the twins are off as well. I was quietly pleased when mum mentioned going up to my sisters for a week, she lives in Bristol. The twins are well happy, it's an adventure for them. I'm staying at home, I got out of it by saying I got so much course work I need to catch up on. The house is gonna be empty so I can get on with it. They seemed to buy it. My mum's so funny, saying things like, 'Are u sure you want to stay, what if something happens and we're not here?' like I'm a kid or something.

'Stop it mum.' Then my dad, 'She'll be fine, she has to learn sooner rather than later'

'Go and enjoy yourself you haven't seen them for ages' I said,

'I'll be all right. When you gonna go?'

My dad turns and says 'We might as well go today'.

'Anne's gonna be well happy to see you guys.'

Mum starts packing before I know it, everything's in the car even the twins, my dad gives me 40 quid. 'Don't tell your mother, shhhhh love you.'

Mum calls out for me to come, passing me some money.

'Na I'm fine mum, thanks doe.'

She kisses me, I can see she doesn't want to leave me but I'm grown now.

'We'll phone you when we get there. Love you.' 'OK' I say, waving them off.

All girls together

Got the house to myself, gonna get all the girls around cook some food, get a draw and a bottle of something, not sure what but strong, really strong, we're gonna get mash up. Everyone en route, I'm gonna do chicken pasta salad. Phoned Naz, he's coming to drop me a draw later, I'll pick up a drink from the corner shop.

Going back to bed for a few hours, can't sleep, text Naz: *come check me at home bring that thing.*

Mum took out some chicken last night, I'll use that. We've got pasta, I find a tin of sweetcorn and I know we have mayo and tomatoes, there's dinner, I think to myself. I season the meat, start chopping up the tomatoes. The door goes, it's Naz.

'Wot's good babe?' he says. 'He's always a happy boy.

'Come man.' I let him in.

'Wot u cooking babes?'

'My girls are coming round, we're gonna catch up.'

'So wot, then can I stay with you lot, bring mans in Jen?'

'Na Naz, it's not one of them nights bruv, next time init.'

'Kool.' He stays for one drink, he's a nutter, always on a girl tip.

His phone goes, he's got to make a move.

'Later. Jen, tell them girls yer you wouldn't let me stay cos I know say you wanna keep me for yourself' (he starts laughing).

'Yep wotever bruv, you're too funny init, go bout ur business.'

I make a cuppa an start frying, the meat it smells so good, the last time I tried to cook dinner I burnt down the house. Look at me now a chef, well training to be one. I'll cook off the pasta later when we're hungry.

Got a text, the girls are all linking up then they're gonna come. I'm really looking forward to seeing them all. Ran myself a bath, put a cd on, had a good long soak, feel better for that. Got dressed just a tracky suit, poured myself a little drink, rolled a fag, nice.

Time's getting on, where are they? With that I can hear them outside, big mouths, I open the door.

'Ello!' kisses flying everywhere.

'We have drink 'Shelly's saying out loud.

'Shut up an get in ere my lovers' (everyone's laughing).

'What's this you're listening to, take it off, we need proper tunes' says Maggie, as she digs though the cds. Oh my god this is a big tune, remember this one?' and we all start singing, drinks in hand.

I'm looking at all my girlies in the same room. We haven't done this for a time, I love it. So Maggie is the dj, she's too pissed to do anything else. Shelly's all loved up, I need to meet this guy, check him out as soon as he touches down. With that I see her hit the floor, I go and help her up. There's a bit of blood on her lip. I take her to the bathroom and clean her up. She's like, 'Jen I love Jason. When he gets here I'm gonna, anyway when we was in, I mean, when I was in Jamaica I saw him every day, I miss him.'

'Did u sleep with him?'

I could see the way she was talkin' bout him, I've seen her with boys before so I dun know she like him. She held my hand.

'Jen it was unbelievable on the beach under the stars, it was magic.'

'But was it what you wanted, I had to make sure?'

'Sure bloody' she replies 'I'll never forget that nite.'

What can I say? As long as he treats her right and she's happy that's all I care about.

We go back to the rest of the girls, Claire's jus got here.

'Wots good babe, you all right Jen? what was all that about the other day, you got me worried.'

'Wot, you couldn't even bell me and let me know you were kool?'

'Sorry babe, was in a bad place.'

'Wot, but everything sorted now yer?' she said, like someone's beefin me or something.

'Yer G, I'm kool.' I don't know if she knows or not, I just want tonight to be nice and forget everything else.

Sonia's lined up some shots, like we haven't had enough already, but we down them anyway. Maggie is dancing like a mad woman, arms and legs all over the place, Shelly's lick out on the sofa, Sonia is drinking in the bath. Don't know how she got there but she's well happy, that leaves Claire and me, Leona couldn't make it. I don't really drink that much but I like a good smoke. We're rollin' up chattin. Sonia was saying she needs to eat, shouting it from the bathroom, so we go to the kitchen. I'm so glad I cooked off the food. all I need to do is the pasta so it will be about 10 mins, nice one babe, the rest of us are smoking, the weed's good man.

Claire is talking about one guy she met, she can get anything she wants out of him, but she don't like him in that way. If her brother ever knew what kinda games she's playing he would go mad, that's not how he wants her to be, like them nasty gals outta road, I don't think so.

'Food's ready.'

Everyone finds themselves in the kitchen, if you ever see the state of em, like animals! It went down nicely though, still smoking hard.

Claire says 'Jen I need to ask you something, come a minute'. We go to my bedroom and shut the door. 'Wot's up babe?'

'Kriss has been talking to me about you.'

'Saying wot?' I felt myself go red.

'How he likes u nuff.'

'Is it?'

'Yer, so wot's going on with you two then?'

'Nothing. Well we kissed, not sure, at the end of the day how would you feel about it if something did happen between us?'

'Jen I just don't want you to get hurt, but the way he's talking about you I think it's for real. He knows how close we are, he wouldn't fuck around, so if that's what you want babe go for it, you're like my sister already I've got nuff love for you.'

Everything's just ah, madness, my head's spinning with it all.

'Don't say nothing to no one not even Kriss, I need to sort things out in my head first' I ask her. I just need a bit of space!

'Kool' and she hugs me, I'm thinking to myself that was nice of her!

We go and join the girls, they're all sleeping. I go and get some blankets to put over them, I feel like the mummy tucking in my babies, swaying all over the place (I'm so mash up). I turn to Claire, she's spread out over the kitchen table, I help her up and take her to the twins' room, put her on Abbie's bed, I've covered her up and left. I did the washing up before heading to bed, then I get a text, *thinkin about you babe x*

That's nice. I remember lying in my bed thinking about everything, smiling.

A new day

The next thing I know it's morning, got nuff missed calls off mum, I better phone her, let her know the girls stayed last night, she'll be fine. At least I weren't on my own.

We're all up now drinking tea, still wrecked from last night, it was well good, had a proper laugh. I'm gonna see Kriss later, have a chat about everything and see where it takes us.

'So wot's everyone on today?' I say.

'I've gotta go home, my dad's back today' says Maggie,

Sonia is going back to Shelly's, she's staying there now, her mum kicked her out. Claire's staying with me until later, she knows I'm gonna link up her brother, I'm so glad she's OK with it all, we will see.

Maggie puts her cup in the sink. 'That's me, I'm gone yer, nice.'

'Wait up Mags we're coming.' Sonia an Shelly put on their coats and head for the front door.

'We have to do it again, I'll bell you guys.'

Shelly and Maggie live on the same street, it's not that far really, last night shows me how much I've missed them.

'Should we get dressed and go to mine?' says Claire.

'Yer, I run a bath.' Claire's going to have a bath at hers, no point in getting washed here, she ain't got no clean underwear.

While I'm getting ready, Claire pops over to the shop to get some fags and some milk, there's none at hers. She comes back. 'You ready Jen?'

'One minute babe.' Just trying to get into this top, it always gives me jip.

As I walk out of the bathroom Claire says, 'You look nice, is that new?'

'Na babe' I reply, 'let's go'. I lock up the house an we're on our way.

We was walking up the road and we had to cut through the flats. As we bust the corner I see a group of people. Claire says 'oh shit, it's Owen.'

'Who's Owen?'

'The guy I've been gettin things off. I was meant to link him the other night but I blew him out.'

'Hey gal wot happen to u, me can't see you.' He's a hard back Jamaican a bit old for Claire I think, she could never like that. She pulls him to the side, says something and he's cool.

'All right, later.'

We start walking. 'Wot did you say to him?' I ask her.

'I told him his luck was in, be ready for my call.'

We're laughing down the road (bennin up). We get to Claire's, she asks me to put the kettle on an drops a big bag of weed on the table. 'Build it when you're ready.'

'Where's that come from babe?' I thought she didn't have anything.

'Owen' she said, like it's nuffin.

'He don't know where you live does he?' Just making sure.

'Na man, imagine Kriss, he would go mad swear down.' She starts laughing.

Claire and Kriss only have each other, their dad left when Claire was a baby. He don't even know what his kids look like, it's a shame cos his children are lovely, he would be so proud at the way they turned out. Then they lost their mum to cancer four years ago, I didn't know them then. I don't know what I would do without my parents, it must have been so hard.

Kriss seems so much older than 21 but he's had to deal with so much, the house, his sister, there's always something to sort out, bills don't pay themselves.

Claire's in the bathroom, Kriss walks in with some shopping.

'Ello babes' he says. I can tell he's pleased to see me, I go an help him with the bags. We're unpacking and putting things away.

'So how have you been?' he asks.

'All I can do is think about you, I can't stop myself.' I'm waiting for him to say something, he just looks at me. I've never seen such a lovely smile.

'So wot then, we gonna go out somewhere, eat something' he says.

'That would be nice' I say, sounding like a chief!

Claire walks in. Happy she's going out, to give Kriss and me sometime on our own. We just click.

He makes me a cuppa, rolls me something to smoke, lights it and hands it to me, he's so caring. Puts on some music and comes and sits next to me, how sweet is that! I'm telling him all about college, there's a girl in my class she's useless, not even joking, I have to do her work for her,

'Why?' he says.

'It's cos I feel sorry for her, everyone take's the mick out of her, she's got spots everywhere.'

By now he's pissing hisself with laughter.

'It's not funny.'

One day we had to watch a short film about bacteria. Jools, that's the girl's name, was on the floor pasted out, and who was she left with, only bloody me.

'That's really funny' he said.

Well it wasn't at the time, let me tell ya.

Blast from the past

'Should we go and get something to eat?' he says.

'Yer come on then.' He's fucking hot man!

He's got a nice car, I know he's up to naughties, he's gotta do what he's gotta do. We're in the car, don't know where we are going. We stop off at the petrol station,

'Do you want a drink babe?' I can see he's up to summit, but I don't care, look at him!

'Can I have a coke please.'

He leans over an kisses me, touching my face. I'm watching him walk in to pay, thinking, you don't even want to know wot's running through my mind. Trust me I need to fix up. Kriss gets back in and passes me the drink.

'Ta babe' I say, we drive off.

'What time do you have to be home babe?'

'Everyone's away.'

'So you can stay out?' He looks round at me with a cheeky grin.

'I'm not easy bruv.'

He starts laughing. 'Did I say anything about that babe? You've got a dirty mind.'

So now we're both laughing. That's what I like about him, we get on so well. I look out of the window, there's fields everywhere.

Kriss says there some rizla and tings in the glove compartment. He pulls up in a lane, I roll up and we share it. He tells me what he's all about. It didn't shock me or anything like that, if anything it bought us closer. He wants to tell me everything, not hiding nuffin.

I already knew he sold weed and other stuff, not silly little draws or nuffin like that, didn't know how deep he was in. He's got mans all over the place working for him, he kept that one hidden. That's good doe, don't let people in ur shit, and that's the kind of person I am, very private.

We start driving, I don't even ask where we are going, I trust him. He puts on a tune and says it reminds him of me, and that I must listen to the words. This guy starts singing about a girl. He doesn't know how to tell her his true feelings, cos he's scared of rejection. As I'm listening I can see Kriss looking at me in such a way girls can only dream about.

'Here we are' he said. I looked up. it's an all nite café. He says it's where he used to come when he was a boy with his mum, they lived up the road. I could see he was a bit upset, I held his hand,

'I miss her so much, she never got to meet you babes, she would have loved you. That's why I thought we could come up here, this place is special to me. So are you, I just want you to know that.'

Bless him, how lucky do I feel? We go in and sit at the table he once sat at with his mum, and he orders the same plate of food he had back then. I join him. We have bacon, eggs, beans and toast plus a cuppa, it was well good, went down a treat.

As we're leaving he says he wants to show me something, we get in the car and drive up the road and he parks up. I can see he's still upset. 'Come babe' I say, with my arms open. As he falls in to me, I can hear him crying,

'Babes' I say. 'It's gonna be all right.' He's had to be so strong for so long now, that's all he knows.

He looks at me, a tear runs down his face, I wipe it away, and hug him so tight. He rubs his hands over my back and I look at him, my heart is racing. We kiss for a few moments and he points at a house. 'That's where I grew up' he says.

We get out of the car and walk over there, Kriss is holding my hand all the way. It's all boarded up so we go round the side of the house. He shows me a picture he carved in the brickwork. He explains that when he was about eight his dog Yella was run over, somehow he got out the back gate. They found him in the morning,

'Do you know babe, he found his way home.'

'Bless him' I say, squeezing his hand just that little bit tighter. We sat on the wall outside and he didn't say a word, just put his arm around me; I've never seen him like that. It was getting a bit cold; we got back in the car and put the heater on. Then Kriss got a phone call.

'I have to take this, sorry babe' he says and he gets out of the car. He walks across the road, I could hear him, he's not happy. I rolled a spliff and put some music on. He was about 10 minutes then he got back in the car. He said 'that's all sorted' and switched off his phone. We just sat chatting for ages about all kinds of things. He's so funny, my sides were splitting.

Then out of the blue he says 'stay with me tonight'. I want to say yes, but I'm not sure I'm ready.

'Na' he says. 'I just wanna hold you in my arms, wake up next to you. We won't do anything you don't want to.' I believe him.

We find a little pub that lets rooms. 'Is this OK babes?' he asks.

'Yer kool' I say. We park up and in we go, it's like I didn't know what to do with myself. We sign in and go to the room, it's nice, a chair in the corner, and a double bed, TV on the wall and a little bathroom, very clean. 'Is this all right babes?' he ask 'coz if not we'll go an find somewhere else.'

'Na I like it, its fine.' I don't know wot to say, never done anything like this.

'Do you wanna grab a drink?' he says. 'We can go down or I'll just go an get it and bring it back up.'

'You go but hurry up' I say. While he's gone I run a bath, get out of my clothes an jump in. It's nice and hot, I'm lying there thinking where is he, then I hear the door shut, Kriss walks in with two glasses, a bottle of Baileys and a draw. He puts the toilet lid down, just sits down, pours a drink and hands it to me. He goes into the bedroom to roll up, I finish up in the bathroom and walk through. Kriss is on the bed, sleeping.

'Babe wake up an get in bed, come on' I say softly. He takes his top off (fucking hell I think to myself), jeans off, we get in bed. I cuddle up to him, he always smells so good, it feels so right, this is where I want to be. He puts his arms around me and holds me tight and we just fall asleep holding each other.

I wake up in the morning to see Kriss watching me.

'Ello babe, you look so beautiful when you're sleeping.'

I smile at him and head to the bathroom. We get ready to make a move, go and pay the bill, we're walking to the car.

'You gonna come back to mine?' Kriss asks.

'Wanna go home and change my clothes first.'

'That's kool' he replies. 'I'll drop you off, why don't you just pick your things up and come back with me?'

'Is that OK, ain't you got things to do?'

'Yer, spend time with you, now I got you there's no lettin go' he said. It's all too good to be true, is this really happening?

We get to mine, grab a few things and leave. Kriss says 'Babe I need to pass by Jay quickly an pick something up.'

I stayed in the car, even though he's told me everything, all that don't do nothing for me, yer kool he's got a nice car but I ain't one of them girls, out for what a man has, with me it's deeper than that. I know nuff people are gonna be like 'she's only with him cos of who he is and what he's got'. That's rubbish, I'm doing things for myself, no man has ever done nothing for me. I've got pride in myself, it's all about the person you know, and he's the nicest person you could ever want to meet, well that's my feeling anyway.

Here he comes, looking hot as always, he gets in the car, kisses me and says 'Let's go home.' He's so sweet, I think to myself. We pull up at his and go inside. He shouts out for Claire, she's sleeping, I put the kettle on. I love my tea, always have done. Kriss is on the phone, cussing someone.

'Babe I need to fly up the road, you're kool here yer, I won't be long this guy's pissing me off, I need to sort it.'

'Yer I'm fine.' He leaves. I can't really say anything, it's what he does, I know the score, he's told me and it's my choice.

While I'm on my own I text mum, *Hiya x hope u guys r OK missing u x* an send.

The saddest things

I put the telly on, I hear his car, I know it's him by the music! I've got butterflies.

He walks in, I'm lying down on the sofa, he comes and lays behind me, puts his arms around me and says 'Wot do you wanna do babe?'

'Can we just stay in, I like being at home?'

'Are you sure? he says, kissing me.

'Yep, just you and me.'

I turn to him and move in to kiss him, his lips are so soft, I so want to take it further, the way I feel about him it takes my breath away. My phone rings.

'Leave it' Kriss says.

'I can't, it might be my mum.'

But I pick up and it's Leona crying, I can't make any sense out of wot she's saying, I'm feelin a bit scared, I try again.

'Where are you babe?'

I hear *hospital*.

'Babe I'm coming.' The phone cuts out.

I turn to Kriss, he grabs his keys. 'Come on let's go.'

All sorts of thing are running though my head, I can't think, it feels like forever before we finally get there. I go to reception and ask if Leona Williams is there, the woman at the desk asks me to wait, then

I see the police!

'Wot's going on, can someone help me?'

A copper makes his way over to me an says 'are you Jennie?'

'Yes, can you please just tell me where Leona is, an if she's OK I need to see her.' He goes on to tell me that he can't go into much detail but she's been hurt badly. I just burst into tears, Kriss is holding me.

'Is she gonna be OK?' I ask.

'We're not sure, they've taken her down for surgery.'

'What happened to her?'

The policeman explains it's a domestic situation. 'We have arrested a young male, but we need to speak to Miss Williams' he says.

A nurse comes over an takes us to a side room. 'You can wait in here, I will keep you up to date.'

'How bad is it?' I ask.

'She's in good hands.' She offers us a drink. No thank you, none of this makes any sense.

I make some calls to see if anyone knows who this guy is. It's like no one knows nothing. I phone the girls and tell them to meet me at kings college, I didn't say what's happened, just get here. About 15 minutes pass, it feels like hours. I can hear voices, I open the door,

Maggie turns around 'U all right?' she says,

'It's Leona man.'

'What? Jen tell me, wot's going on!'

I tell her as much as I know. With that in walks Shelly an Sonia, Shelly's been crying. Maggie's angry, well we all are, Shelly can't stop herself.

'That's why she didn't come the other nite' she said wiping her eyes,

'Wot do you mean, do you know something? I swear down, Shelly speak.'

I'm not even joking she can see by my face; I'm not fucking about, Leona's in there fighting for her life.

'I'm waiting.' You see how I have to talk to her.

'She met some guy a few months ago.'

'Where?' I say.

'I don't know Jen.'

'Wot's his name?'

'Marcus I think. I told her something about him weren't right, but you know her, she doesn't listen to no one.'

'Why didn't you say anything?'

'She made me promise not too.'

Maggie got up and flew at her. 'Leave her' I said, 'that's not helping anyone.'

We sit and wait. That's all we can do. Kriss is outside making some calls, seeing if some of his boys know this guy. Leona's mum walks in and sits down, she's so upset I go and sit with her, she tells us she ain't seen Leona since she meet him.

'Have you met him mum?' That's what we call her.

'Na she wouldn't bring him to the house, now I see why. I talked to her on the phone, I could hear this man in the background saying things like, see you, yer fucking useless and shit like that.'

'I just tell her come home, but she never reach and now look.'

The doctor comes in, and explains everything went well. She has 5 stab wounds, 4 to the upper body and 1 to the lower body, she's had a blow to the back of the head, that she is stable and we can go and see her but not for long, they're gonna keep her in. I go in with her mum, she's black and blue and it doesn't even look like the girl I know. I had to get out of there, seeing her like that shook me, I hate hospital at the best of times.

The police want to speak to me,

'Jennie' he said, 'Can you shed some light as to what happened tonight?'

'I've known Leona for years officer, the guy I only found out about him today.'

He looks at me. 'Is that the truth?'

'Yer.'

'You're not going to do anything silly are you?'

'What do you mean, I thought you said you've nicked him?'

'Yes he's at the police station now, he will go down for this.'

I leave and go to find Kriss. I see him sitting on a bench outside.

'Can we go babe?'

I tell him everything, he puts his arm round me, I feel safe. 'Where do you want to go?' he says.

'Back to yours if that's OK, I need something to smoke.' My draw's there.

What a day, it started out so nice and ended so shit, but Leona's gonna be OK, that's the main thing.

On our way to the car Kriss stops me. 'I've made some calls, I'll find him, don't worry it will get sorted babe.'

'When you do find him, I don't want you to do nuffin, just let me know where he is, I can sort it out myself.' She's my girl, I will do what needs to be done.

I didn't mean anything by it! He looks at me like wot the fuck are you saying? I can look out for myself, I would never put him in any danger. One day I will let him into who and what I'm really about, but right now I just want to be with him and forget everything, just for tonight. I never thought I would find anyone on my level. Kriss is a male version of me.

The things we have to deal with

We're in the car, and he says 'Wot did you mean, you can sort it?'

'Kriss, there are things you don't know about me,'

'Like wot?' he says.

'I don't know, I'm a bit naughty.'

We've all done things you know. But a man who does things like that you gotta deal with them right, beating is too good for him.

Kriss pulls me to him, the kiss is electric. I don't know how much longer I can keep my hands off him. We drive to the house, I get a call off Maggie, she's gonna meet me at mine in an hour; you see how quick things can change. I say 'Kriss, I have to go.'

'Where?'

'Home.' Can things get any worse?

'Do you want me to drop you babe?'

'Na I need the fresh air, clear my head.'

I say my goodbyes. On the way to the door Kriss calls out 'Babe, bell me when you're done.'

I turn and see his face and blow him kisses, wotever I do, I've got to do it right. I get home and put the heating on, it's bloody cold in here, make myself a cuppa. That's better, roll a fag and sit and wait.

Tick Tock

All kinds of madness is running through my head and now I've got to deal with Maggie. The doorbell goes. I'm not looking forward to this. I let them in, Maggie starts straight away.

'We gotta deal with this fam, mans need to get fucked up, why didn't any of us know wot was going on with Leona?'

'If we do this we do it right, Shelly. You said you met the dude yer? So you know wot he looks like.'

'Yer' Shelly says,

'Wot do you mean, yer?'

Maggie starts 'If you would have opened your mouth in the first place, Leona wouldn't be in the fucking hospital stabbed up would she, you dumb bitch!'

'Don't man' I say, 'we all need to be together on this.'

Maggie carries on 'Na star, you fucked up, I heard you say the guy weren't right and you did nuffin, you just fucking left her there, you make me fucking sick.'

'Shut the fuck up this ain't helping no one, I want everyone to go home, I'm going to get some things in play and I'll holla.'

If Maggie had her own way it would be dealt with tonight, but my man is locked up safe and sound, the only way to do this is bide our time, get me? I text Kriss, *babe can you come pick me up* I don't wanna be by myself.

The girls leave, I hear a car horn, I look out of the window, its Kriss. That's wot I'm saying, when I need him he's there. I lock up and get in the car. He looks at me and says, 'So what happened?'

I tell him Shelly met him one time.

'Where?' he says.

One drink, little while ago.

'Didn't you go?' he asks.

'Na, that weekend my uncle David passed away.' I remember he died on the Thursday, them lot went out on the Friday.

'But anyway Maggie wanted to beat her up.'

'Who?' he's so slow sometimes.

'Shelly! she knew the guy weren't right, and still said nuffin.'

But to tell you the truth she was in Jamaica, doing her own thing after that.

We get to his, I'm so tired, I sit on the sofa, my belly's rumbling

'You hungry babe?'

'Na, could I just have tea?'

I don't know what happened, I wake up at like 3 am and I can hear Kriss on the phone. I get up an go into the front room where he is.

'Ello babe, wot you doing up?'

'I can't sleep' I say, walking over to him. He has the phone in one hand and he's reaching for me with the other. 'I've gotta go' he says and he hangs up.

We just stand there cuddling, holding each other. He takes my hand and walks me to the bedroom, I'm thinking to myself wot's he doing, I'm not feeling this right now?

He goes to a drawer and opens it, and takes out a bag of weed. I smile, trust me I was so glad it was that and nuffin else. He put on some music really low, we could just about hear it. We smoke the night away.

He's not like other guys, not out for what he can get. Sometimes I look at him and want him so much, but for wotever reason I can't go there. I was seeing someone, he cheated on me and got a next girl pregnant. I really checked for him, that hurt me nuff, my trust has gone in men, but I don't feel like that with Kriss, so I'm gonna take one day at a time and see where that takes us.

In the morning I go to the hospital, to see how Leona's doing. I don't go in just leave flowers. I go back to mine, the house is so empty. I put the heating on and fall asleep watching telly.

I must have been sleeping for hours coz when I wake up it's dark outside. I sit for a few minutes, then get up to make something to eat,

I put a pizza in the oven, I make myself a cuppa and try to do some course work but it's not sinking in, I'll have to do it later.

Pizza's ready, a bit burnt but it will do me, I'm bloody starving. As I'm eating my phone rings, it's my mum.

'How you are darling, is everything all right?'

'Yer I'm fine, missing you guys, when you coming home?'

'Well if it's OK with you we're gonna stay on for another week.'

'Oh OK then.'

Mum asks how my course work's going. 'Fine' I reply, wish I went with them now. We say bye and hang up. I just curl up on the sofa, didn't know how much I was gonna miss them.

I wake up to my phone ringing, its Maggie, I can't deal with her right now. I let it ring out, she's doing my head in, always wanting to be inner hype.

I run a bath and just lie there trying to clear me head, the bloody door's going, I ignore it, than I hear Maggie. I get out of the bath and go to the door.

'Maggie man, wot you doing?'

She comes in, I leave her in the front room while I go an get dressed,

'Can I make a coffee?' she asks.

'Help yourself, there are some biscuits on the table I'll be out in a minute babe. I come back in the room, Maggie's just sitting there looking at me,

'Wot?' I ask her.

'Wot's the plan?'

'Maggie the fucking guy's in nick plan, wot fucking plan?'

'Have you even been to see her?' It's like I'm talking to myself.

'Maggie what the hell are you doing here?'

'I can't let this go Jen, wot we gonna do?' It's like talking to a brick wall.

'What do you want me to say?'

'I don't want you to say anything, I want us to deal with this, sort this shit out.'

'Maggie, do you understand the guys fucking locked up, you need to go home now, me and you are gonna fall out.'

'Why?' she says,

'Coz you don't hear, I said it will get sorted.' She takes too much drugs, she don't know if she's coming or going.

'I'll phone you, I've got places to be right now.'

'Where?' She's too inner man!

'Don't ask me my business.'

We leave. I just wanna get rid of her. I get to the station and ask for PC Whitmore, then I sit and wait.

'Hi Jennie do you want to follow me?' He takes me to an interview room; I didn't even give him time to breath. 'What's happening can you tell me?'

'The male we arrested is up in court tomorrow morning, he won't get bail, he's up for attempted murder, he'll go away for a long time.'

I ask what court, he won't tell me, I do understand. Fair play, I wouldn't tell me either. I'm a firm believer in wot goes around comes around.

I thank him for his time. I don't know why but I jump on a train, don't even know where it's going, I don't really care, anywhere away from here.

I get off at Hounslow East and start walking. It's nice up there, big fuck-off houses, they gotta be worth a million at least, one day that will be me. I make my way back, gonna stop off at the hospital, I get off the train at Vauxhall. I can pick up the 436 to Kings. Standing waiting for the bus, thinking about when us lot were little and we became blood sister, that was so funny it took us all day. We did it though and we swore to always be there for each other no matter wot.

My bus pulls up, someone shouts out Jen, I look round, it's Andy, he's on my course.

'You all right?' I say.

'Wot do you live around here?'

'Up the road.' I don't even like him, he's a wanker.

'This is my stop, later yer, I'll see you at college.'

I was glad to get off the bus, I'm not in the mood for them. I can see the hospital, I walk across the road, don't even know who's gonna be there. I'm dreading it, hate the smell of these places, full of sick people. I get to the ward and pull back the curtain,

'Hi babe' I say. She's still looking a bit ruff. How you feeling? She smiles.

'A lot better.'

I go right into it. 'Wot happened fam?'

She starts crying,

'I thought he was gonna kill me, he just flipped out Jen, I couldn't do anything to stop it, I was so scared.'

I get on the bed and comfort her. 'It's gonna be all right hun.' I can see she's holding back on something?

'The police came today, he's up in court tomorrow.'

'They said he won't get bail, but wot if?'

'Don't' i say?

'Either way he's gonna get his, all I want is for you to get better yer, don't worry it's all in hand.'

I stay a little while, well until Leona falls asleep. I kiss her and leave. I end up walking home, thinking about all kinds of stuff. At home I make a bed up in the front room, when I was little my mum would do that for me (I miss her). I put a dvd on and just chill. The film's playing, but you know when you're watching it but you don't see it? I couldn't even tell you wot it was about or who was in it, just one of them days.

Leona on my mind

I wake up early, Leona's on my mind and the hardest thing about it all
is that I can't do anything about it right now, it's a waiting game. I phone
Claire, I'm gonna link her later, I like her, we've done a few naughty
moves together, I can trust her. I need to be prepared for the worst,
you know wot the law's like, people get away with all sorts of things.
Not on my watch, he best hope he stays in jail. Sometimes I have off
key thoughts, like how to really hurt a person, I mean torture, to the
brink of death. If I ever get my hands on this fucking guy, his life won't
be worth living, let me tell ya. I've always been a bit twisted, got anger
deep down inside, it's hard keeping it under wraps.

My phone rings, it's Claire. 'Can you bring some fags? Wot time you
reaching me babe?'

'About an hour, see you in a bit.' I go and get ready, and leave.

I stop off at the corner shop,

'Morning Ali, could I have 10 Mayfair and a small blue rizla.'

'How's the family.' he asks. He tells me his wife has taken the kids
to Portsmouth to her sisters, for half term, and he's enjoying the peace
and quiet. We're laughing, he's a nice man always got time for a chat.
He asks where my mum is, saying she hasn't been in to get the paper
for a while,

'Yer, they've gone up to Bristol to see my sister.' I say bye and leave, 'places to go people to see' I'm saying as I'm walking out the door. I light a fag and start walking, it's not far, gotta sort out things with Claire, I know she's gonna be up for it, wotever it is.

Got a text off Claire, *where u at g x* Sent one back, *outside open the door x*

'Where's your brother Claire?'

'Not ere he's somewhere doing summit.' For true she don't even know.

'Do you want tea babe?' she asks.

'Yes please.'

'Claire we got to talk, I don't want anybody knowing nuffin, but if this guy gets bail we know what we're doing yer?'

'Wot for true Jen, we're doing this thing.'

'Damn right, my man can't walk away from this, he could have killed Leona, he's taking the fucking piss.'

We're smoking, and drinking tea, Claire's like, 'So if he gets bail, wot's happening?'

'Don't worry' I say,' I will sort everything out, I just need to know you're with me on this.'

'Yer of course fam.'

'Right when I leave here, I'm gonna see Veronica.' That's Leona's mum.

'See wot happened at court, and take it from there.'

'I'm coming 'Claire says.

'Kool but hold it down yer? I don't want anyone knowing nuffin, I mean no one. Let's have one more cuppa then we'll make a move.'

We get to the house,

'Hi mum. I can see she's sad. 'Wot happened at court?' I ask giving her a cuddle.

'Jen' she says holding me tight. 'His lawyer made out like it was all Leona's doing.'

'Wot you sayin mum?'

She carries on to say it was a drugs deal that went wrong and he never touched her, he said they owe so many hundred pounds and that the dealers want their money, and because they didn't have it, they started stabbing her, like she was nothing, he's saying that he had to beg and took a beating hisself.

'So wot then, did he look beat up mum?'

'No Jen he has to be laying the way he was, it was creepy. Jen I'm going to ask you something.'

'Yes mum anything what's on your mind.' I'm just hoping I've got the answer for her.

'Do you girls take drugs'?

'Mum man!'

'Well do you'!

'We smoke weed, that's it, why you asking that.'

'Coz he's saying Leona's on crack.'

'Come on mum he's trying to save his own skin, but it not gonna work they will see through him. We just gotta be there for Leona. When she coming home?'

'In a few days, will you come?'

'Yer course I will, you don't have to ask.'

I keep catching Claire looking at me, we stay awhile then leave, we don't even discuss it. We head over to Naz's house, he's always on a joke ting, that's why we like it there. Something's always happening, the people, the vibes nice, never no trouble. We knock the door and as it opens we hear Naz say, 'I hope this is some hotties coming to check me. Jen and Claire, wot's good ladies, couldn't stay away, come man.'

'Wot's good bruv? Always looking gal init.'

'Wot you sayin' Jen? You're looking hot doe as always.'

'Fix up bruv, you could never handle this, I'm out of your league.'

'Don't knock it till you try it' he says, smiling. With that he starts on Claire, watch him! 'Claire, wot you sayin' babe, you are all I need trust.'

We all start laughing, a man can hope init? He's always liked me but I see him as a brother, no more no less.

We go into the front room. 'Wot's good?' I look I say that's Danni, Naz' cuz. He's really nice lookin' but his nose just don't go with his face, but as a person he's blinding in every way, good Indian boys they are.

'This is Claire' I say. We go and sit down.

'Do you lot wanna drink?'

'Yer, can I have tea?' I ask hoping he will make it.

'Kool' he replies. 'Claire?'

'You got summit strong?' She's too fast. Naz goes and gets a bottle, he only comes back with brandy. Claire's like 'Yep that's wot I'm talkin about'. She pours herself a drink and rolls a joint.

Naz calls me to the kitchen and shuts the door.

'Jen don't take this the wrong way but I see Leona's mum, and she told me what happened, mans outta road trying to find this guy, but I feel say mans off the ends.'

'I know Naz it's hard man, you've known me for years so you dun know wot I'm about, I ain't lettin' this one go.'

'That's wot I'm sayin Jen, if you need anything.' He grabs my arm.

'Anything you come to me yer? Mans will sort that shit'. He steps closer and says in a quiet voice, 'Anything you need I can get, understand?'

You don't know how good it was to hear that. 'You gotta hold it down Naz, don't mention this to no one.'

'Na kool babe, no more said, come let's smoke, I've got some good green. Jen, roll up out of this one.'

Naz loves his green boy, the names of some of them swear down they just make them up, Claire's not easy she smokes like it's going out of fashion.

'Slow down Claire' I say.

'Na I need this, you know I do.' We ain't moving for now anyway.

My phone rings, it's Kriss. 'Hiya babe you all right?' He tells me he's fine and that he misses me, that's nice.

'I miss you too, when am I gonna see your face babe?' I let him know I'm with his sister and that she's all right, we say our goodbyes and hang up.

'Who was that?' Claire asks, Kriss I say.

'When is he due back?'

'Next week some time, I've missed him.'

'Wot's that Jen, you and Kriss is that you yer?'

'Shut up Naz.'

'I'm just asking a question' he says, looking kinda shady.

'When there's something to tell you'll know init, now I'm gonna get lean up kool.'

'Safe Jen.'

So I'm sitting there not really paying attention to no one, everyone's catching joke.

That's life

I remember when all of us were inseparable, I don't understand why Leona kept things from us. Well that's a lie, she wouldn't tell me coz I would have put a stop to it from the start. She knows no man should ever put his hands on no gal, woman wotever, no one has that right.

We end up leaving Naz about 2 am mash up. We took a cab back to Claire's, we were wrecked. When we got there I just found my way and went to bed, I slept in Kriss's room. As soon as my head hit the pillow I was off.

I've fallen for him. He's not having to know my every move, who I'm with wot I'm doing, that's the way I like it.

I wake up early. It's a bit strange being in Kriss's room on my own. I go an make a cuppa and go back to lay down, I wrap myself in the blanket and close my eyes. I wish I could be this good girl Kriss needs, when I'm with him that's how I wanna be, that's who I am, but now this thing with Leona's taking me somewhere I don't want to go, but I have to.

If I do it right no one has to ever know. It's all too much, I've found something in Kriss I don't want to lose? But on the other hand I can't let this Marcus guy get away with it, so much stuff is running through my mind. I put the radio on low and just doze.

I wake up to Claire tickling my face with her pony tail, giggling to herself. 'You're such a chief' I say to her,

'Leave it out I don't like it, you fool.'

'Jen, move over.'

She jumps in the bed, we lay there chatting.

'So that thing Jen, I can get handcuffs, proper tings no one's getting out of them believe that fam.'

'Where from?' I say (still feelin a bit sleepy).

'My little links' she replies.

'Kool, everything else leave to me yer?' But for true they will come in handy, trust. We go and make tea and roll up. Nothing planned for today waiting on a few phone calls, to see when Leona's due home from the hospital. In the front room just chillin.

'Jen wot's going on with you an Kriss?'

'We're taking it slow, I know it's him I want to be with.'

She's looking at me, I can't hide any more.

'I've been hurt before, and it weren't fucking nice' I say. I try and make her understand. 'With your brother you're in that, an this Leona thing, things are nuts right now. I don't want to get inner your family then fuck it all up, once things are sorted then I can look at me and Kriss, I will talk to him when I see him.'

'He really likes you Jen.'

'Yer me too, more then I'm letting on.'

'So you're not ending things with him?' she says, looking unsure of my answer.

'No way babe, are you not hearing me? I've fallen for him in a big way. I need to be up front with him, I suppose he will do what's best for him.' I'm hoping she understands.

'He's not like that Jen, he knows wot your about, he's heard certain things about you. It's a small world. He's asked me stuff, things we've done, things you've done, he fucking knows the lot fam, he ain't going nowhere you'll see.'

'I hope so.' I wanted to be the one to tell him everything, well he's heard second hand so that means nothing, you know how people love to chat shit.

'I wonder wot he thinks of me.'

'Jen he wants to be with you, everything's gonna be kool.'

We go into the kitchen. 'What do you fancy to eat Jen?'

'You got any bacon?'

'Yer,' Nice one, I reply, Claire's doing the food. I'm making the tea and rolling up.

'Put some music on Jen.'

'Wot do you want to listen to?' I shout through

'Anything babe, put the radio on, let's see wot's happening in the world today.'

She's like an old woman sometimes.

'Turn it up I love this one.' She's bopping round the place like an octopus, arms and legs that's all I can see, I love her, she don't business wot she looks like. Leona is never far from my thoughts though, I try an keep it down. The radio is bangin out tune after tune.

'Do you want any sauce on your sandwich?'

'Na you're all right, I'll have it as it comes, thanks babe.'

Nice and crispy that's how I like it. I swear that was the best bacon sandwich, it had like seven bits of bacon in their, baby gem and tomato, it was wicked.

My phone goes, it's Veronica, letting me know Leona is due home tomorrow, she has to have some tests done and as long as everything's fine their letting her home early.

'Kool mum' I say.

'We'll be there, I'll let her settle in for a bit. Do you need me to bring anything for you mum?'

'No just bring yourself, see you soon.'

That's what I'm saying, it's one thing after another.

I like a nice quiet life, I'm not into people's business, I like things on a nice even keel but it don't always work out that way. I used to be one of them girls outta road not like that, I mean movin' with the wrong people, you don't see it when your init, getting into all sorts of shit on the odd occasion, havin to fuck someone up. I'm not really like that but you know how things are sometimes, you have to stand up and do your thing. I thought them days were long gone, then summit happens and it all changes.

I turn to Claire. 'Leona's getting' home about 3 tomorrow.'

'So do we know anything yet?'

'I know he's going up for bail, we'll have to wait and see. I will keep you in the loop, but when things kick off I don't want you there babe.'

'Wot you fucking nuts Jen? Stop chatting shit fam, we're in this together, I've got your back about not coming so wot you sayin'?'

I look at her and tell her as it is. 'Wot didn't you hear me, I'm not fucking about, you ain't gonna be there!'

'You can't do it by yourself.' It's like she ain't listening.

'I'm kool, I know what I'm doing.'

'Wot are you doing?' she asks

'Don't watch that babe, everything's in hand, don't you get it, the less you know the better.'

'I'm not like that, go run to people for help. I learnt a long time ago to stand on my own two feet, you know like when you put your trust in someone and you believe in them you let them in to your deepest darkest thoughts, things you done good or bad whatever it was or wasn't, and then when things come to the crunch they shit all over you, I've been there I know first-hand. Not saying you're like that coz I know you ain't, I just don't want you involved.'

'You know me babe, I've gone on moves on my own before, remember I used to move with them mans. I'm not stupid, I done worst things so trust me when I say I know what I'm doing.'

I can see Claire has the hump, but in time she'll know it was for the best keeping her out of it. My mum always says the only person you should ever trust is that person looking back at you in the mirror, and I live by that. I trust certain people in my life to a limit, always hold a bit back, never give your all, coz when summit happens that's when you know who your people are, so it's just best to stand on your own.

'Claire man' I say.

'Jen it's kool, I know what you're saying, it's because you care, I can see that but I'm worried about you.'

'Don't be babes, you know me, hard as nails when I have to be' I say as I give her a cuddle. I go and have a bath and get dressed. I tell Claire I'm gonna fly up the road quickly.

'I soon come' I say as I shut the door. Need to see Leona so I head to the hospital.

The truth

When I get there she's not in her bed. I ask the nurse.

'It's OK she's gone down to x-ray, you can wait for her' she said.

I go and wait. I need to know everything that happened and I need it to be the truth. I flick through one magazine. I look up and there's Leona. I smile. She looks a lot better than the last time I saw her.

'Hiya babe' I say. She looks a bit shocked to see me.

'You all right Jen?'

'Yer I'm kool, how you feeling?'

'I'm fine, wot you been up to?'

'Not a lot, you know how it is, I see your mum the other day. Wot's going on fam, and you best not leave nuffin out, get me?'

'Going on with wot Jen?'

'All right Leona, why is your mum asking me if you're on crack fam?'

'Wot do you mean Jen?'

'Don't take me for a fool yer? Just say it as it is init.' I didn't even want to look at her, cos I wanna know everything and she won't tell me if I watch her.

'All right then, I met him at one drink up, you weren't there doe, he was nice. We linked up a few times, I liked him.'

'So why didn't you tell anyone?'

'Shelly knew, she came out with us.'

45

'Is it? so wot happened that night?'

'I met him up Oxford Street, we went for a coffee. He seemed a bit on edge. I asked him what was up and he said he had had a really bad day but he was all right, we walked and talked. Everything was nice, we jumped on the bus'

'Where does he live?'

'North London, anyway we get off the bus and he seemed kool, reached his house everything still fine, he got a phone call then the mood changed. He screamed at me, started saying I'm a fucking dirty little slag. I was trying to calm him down asking him why he saying that, you know why you fucking little bitch, the way he looked at me Jen I was getting scared.'

'Go on.'

'The next thing I know he's in my face with his hands around my throat, spit flying out of his mouth, his eyes man, fucking hell I was shitting myself I ain't even gonna lie, I was crying telling him to let go. He punch me in the face then went mad he punched me that hard I was lifted off the floor. He must have knocked me out, coz all I remember was seeing him standing over me with a knife. I shouted at him not to, I was begging him not to, but he just started stabbing me, at first he stabbed me in my leg and as he was doing it, do you know what he said, that's so you can't leave me! Sick man he's fucking twisted Jen!'

I'm sitting listening to my mate taking me through a blow by blow account of her nearly dying, wot the fuck!

'I don't recall anything after that' she says. 'Well, apart from waking up at the hospital.'

'So let me get this clear, things were kool with you and him?'

'Well na they weren't, he just used to freak out for no reason.'

'Why the fuck did you hang around then?'

'I liked him, that's all I can say, it won't happen again.'

'So were you two on crack?' I had to ask her.

'Na, he took it.' she said with her head down.

'And you?'

'I tried it but it's nasty, I didn't like it, I just smoked weed.'

'So he's went nuts on you and stabbed you up, is that what you're telling to me?'

'Yes Jen.' She's crying. bless her.

'Sorry babe, I needed to know, get things clear in my mind, you know I love you.'

'Yer babe.'

'Do you know his address?'

'Wot do you want it for?'

'Just write it down for me.'

'Jen...'

'Don't even say it.'

I take the paper, kiss her.

'I'm coming to check you tomorrow.'

'I'm going home tomorrow.'

'Yer I know, I mean at your house, but I gotta go now. See you soon, don't worry babe, everything is gonna be all right.'

I leave and walk to the bus stop. As I'm standing there I'm watching people everywhere going about their business, not a care in the world, and then there's me. I feel so out of place, I feel I could tear someone's face off. I'm a bit pissed off. how can a man treat a woman like that? He's gonna fucking pay big time, I don't give a fuck who you are or where you're from, don't get me wrong, I'm kool. I would help anyone, but mess with the ones I love and that's it all over, I'm a fucked-up bitch you would never wanna meet.

I don't think like everyday people. If it was back in the day I would be runnin tings out ere right about now. Gangster's moll? I would have been the gangster, I've got a sick side. Haven't we all?

On the bus watching one man with his little kids, they look so cute but boy you never know what's round the corner. My parents ain't got a clue to what I'm about, they just see what I want them to see. One golden rule, never shit on your own door step. Ever.

Wastegal

I get off the bus and walk around to Claire's, it's like less than 5 mins. My phone rings. It's Naz.

'Wot good bruv?' I say.

'Jen can you come to mine? Now Maggie's ere and she's on one, man.'

'I'm on my way, keep her there yer?'

We all live on the same manor, so it's handy to breeze in and out, one to the other.

So I reach Naz's yard, I knock the door, I can hear whole heap of commotion inside. The door opens.

'Wot's going on?' I say (Naz looks pissed off).

'Fuckin hell Jen man, wot the fuck is wrong with that girl? I swear down you need to sort her out star.'

'Where is she?'

He points to the front room. I push the door and there's Maggie, fucking hanging off her face, chatting shit. I walk over to her.

'Wot the fuck are you doing?' I say.

She gets up right in my face, smelling nasty and that. 'Wot the fuck do you want?'

'Wot, you fucking dumb bruv, who you fucking talking too, wot you doing here? how you coming here in that state, what's wrong with you?'

She said nuffin.

'So wot, you not talkin now? Na, nuffin to say big mouth, I tell you wot yer you best go home and fix up.'

'Na.' That's how I know she's mash up. I'll knock her out.

'Wot do you mean na, you're starting to really piss me off, what then you got summit to say!'

It was quiet for a minute then she said 'Wot's happening with Leona and this thing Jen? It's like no one's tellin me anything, wot's that about?'

'I'll tell ya this ting with Leona is all in hand, yer, and you, you're a fucking liability. You take too much drugs, drink too much, you're a waste of fucking air right now, I can't fuckin trust you, look at you, you're a joke! Do you really think that this is what Leona needs right now? It's hard enough for her, she don't need all your shit on top of everything, so yer that's right I don't need that sort of help. Now you need to go home, you ain't no good to no one like that.'

She gets up and walks to the door, I tell her to leave things alone. I make it very clear I don't want to hear nuffin and ask her if she understands wot I'm saying to her.

'Yer Jen, I hear you.'

I don't trust her, summit telling me I need to watch her. They say there's a thin line between love and hate. Maggie is my girl but sometimes I wish I never knew her.

She thinks she a bad girl, same old shit just another day that's wot my life is filled with right about now, everything seems to be going downhill fast I feel all alone with the weight of the whole on my little shoulders, I just sit there thinking how did I get here, college is going so well an then there's Kriss maybe he's the right person at the wrong time, wot the fuck am I gonna do. I so want him in my life, wish he was ere now to give me one of them cuddles I feel so safe with him, he dose summit to me he's infectious

'Jen you all right mate'

'Yer Naz Maggie's doing my head in, I don't know what's wrong with her, I'm sorry for that bruv you need to stop her from coming here.'

'Na Jen I ain't even seen her, swear.'

'Wot, she don't get her draws from you na?'

'Na babes.'

'Na babes, I think she's on more than that you see her, weed doesn't do you like that she on some different shit.'

Maggie is always up and down but there's other people out there who's had shit done to them, they just get on with life the best they can, but this girl is dangerous. Right now she's high most of the time, I can't watch her every move, but then again she's so fucking out of it people won't take her seriously, to them she's just another druggy?

'Naz I gotta go bruv, if she comes back bell me, yer?'

I give him a hug and leave en route to Claire's, its kinda cold out here so I finally get there as Claire opens the door. She's like, 'where you been?'

'Had to pop by Naz, Maggie turned up out of it, she's really pissin me off, hotting up everything.'

'Why wot she sayin?'

'Nuffin really, but she's on this Leona ting, fair play luckily she went to Naz but I don't know wot she's been sayin outta road, who she's been talking, I don't know wot do her, I had to tell her to back off.'

'Is it' Claire says.

'Yer man, if anything else happens I might have to grip her up, I don't wanna have to step to her but if I need to trust I will.'

'Do you want tea babe, are you gonna stay tonight?'

'Na i need to pass by Delroy (that's Maggie's dad) see if he's noticed anything, he might be able to tell me wot's going on with her, who she's been moving with, but yer, a quick cuppa before I go will be nice.'

'Do you want me to come?' Claire asks.

'Na babe, I won't be there long, then I'm gonna go home got to try catch up with some college work.' I finish my tea and get ready to leave.

'Jen, you sure you don't want me to come with you babe?'

'Na hun you're kool.' I give her a hug and go.

I take the short cut, it's a bit dark, nuff youts hanging round. It's kool, I know them, but I don't like it when I see them on road till all hours, they're young, they should be at home.

I reach Delroy's, don't look like anyone's in, I lost my phone a few weeks ago, it had his number in it. I'm knocking the door, no answer so I knock and wait a minute, no one. I'll pass tomorrow I think to myself and walk away. As I'm shutting the gate the door opens.

'Jen, all right?'

'Evenin Delroy.'

'Maggie's not here' he says.

'Na I haven't come to see her, I need to talk to you if you're not busy.'

'Come in, come man' he says. We go into the front room.

'So what's up?' he says.

'How's Maggie doing?' I say. Don't want to give too much away.

'Jen you know we've fallen out, I ain't seen her for a few days.'

'What do you mean, Delroy?'

'Well she come in 'ere cussing, smashing my place up, she took money outta my wallet, she don't respect anything. If she wasn't my daughter I would have knock her out, she's too bloody rude'

'Shit, is that how it is for true?'

'Yer Jen I've just had enough of her, I can't do it any more. So if you do see her tell her she ain't welcome ere.'

'Shit Delroy, I'm sorry man.'

'Do you know wot's going on with her Jen?'

'Summit happened to Leona, maybe that's it.'

'Yer, but it's always something with her, no one else is like it. She just takes tings too far man, I'm sick of her.'

'Where she staying?'

'I don't know and I don't care.'

'Well I've got to go now.'

'OK nice to see you Jen, say hello to the family for me,'

'Will do, later.'

At home, the house is so quiet and cold. I put the heating on and fill the kettle, set up my cup and go get my dressing gown and slippers, put the telly on and chill for a bit before getting stuck in my books. I miss my mum, it feels like they've been away for ages. I roll a joint. I don't wanna be this person any more, sometimes it feels like I'm drowning. I just smoke myself to sleep and hope tomorrow's a better day.

I wake up at like 5 am, make tea and do my course work, it was bloody easy. I think I just needed a clear head. So glad that's all done. I do the dusting and tidy up. It's so quiet, I hate it. I put the radio on and make something to eat, then run myself a bath.

Leona's home today. I wonder what that's gonna bring. I need to get summit off her anyway. It's still early, so I go back to bed for a bit. I don't know what happened.

I wake up to the door knocking, I get up and answer it, it's Claire.

'Wot you doing Jen, its 2.30?'

'Swear down, I was up so early this morning. Come man. I'll put some clothes on. Make me a tea please babe.'

'Kool' she says. 'Wot you doing with all this stuff?'

'College, man. I've been trying to do it for days now, just couldn't get my head round it, but for some reason I got up early today and done it one time.'

'Nice one' she says. I walk into the front room and have my cuppa.

'I don't wanna reach there too early, all the family will be passing through, we're leave it a bit. You got rizla, babe?' Claire asks.

'In my room' I say. She goes and gets it and we roll up.

'So what's the plan' says Claire.

'I was thinking about everything yer? She must have photos of him on her phone and his number, I'll find out where he moves. I've got his address but I don't just want to go there, I need to find out what he's about first.'

We stay at mine for a bit smoking, go to the chip shop and then back home.

'You got brown sauce Jen?'

'Yep let me get it.' I grab two cokes as well. We sit down and eat.

'So wot happened with Delroy last night babe?'

'Boy, if you ever heard him star, he don't want nuffin to do with her, he said if she weren't his daughter he would knock her out.'

'Shut up Jen!'

'Swear down, he's kicked her out and everything.'

'So wot then, where she staying?'

'He said he don't know and he don't care an that she ain't welcome at his no more.'

'Shit fam, for true?' Claire can't believe it. That's her dad you know, so wot's other people gonna be thinking? (she's a waste, man.) You know that old saying, wot goes around comes back around, that's wot happens when you fuck up!

'I've eaten too make, my tummy's hurting me.'

'Do you need a toilet?' she says.

'I'm not a kid Claire, fuckin heck!' We laugh.

'Wot time do you wanna reach Leona's?' Claire asks.

'About 5 ish, hope that gal don't turn up.'

It's just one thing after another

We're watching the telly, the news is on. They're talking about one guy who got stabbed to death. When they put his photo up I couldn't believe it, it's my ex! The one who cheated on me an got that gal pregnant, there's that saying again! (Apparently they got the wrong person.)

'I don't buy it, he was mixed up with some fuckry people, I heard a little summit about him awhile back but I didn't think nuffin of it the time.'

'Wot?' says Claire. 'Are you sure it's him though?'

'Yer man it is, it's got summit to do with that gal, I told him at the time. He didn't want to be with her, he stayed for the baby's sake, but stayin for the kids never works.'

'So wot did you hear?'

'Have you heard of a guy called Topper?'

'Topper, na fam... yer I have, dark-skinned yout.'

'That's the one, he's safe, but if he don't know you, he could be a right cunt, do you know wot I mean?'

'Oh my god' says Claire.

'Yer that's wot I'm sayin. Anyway that little piece of skirt that Arron got up the duff, well that was Topper's ting, he broke her when she was like 12 blood.'

'Shut up!'

'Swear down, so to him that's his! But he handled her harsh, she weren't allowed anywhere, he used to bring his boys round just to fuck her.'

'Fucking hell wot you sayin, how you know all this?'

'I used to move with him still, time ago! He always said I was a fool being with Arron but you don't see it at the time, do ya?'

With that my phone rings.

'Hello?'

'Hi, is this Jennie?'

'Yep, who's that?'

'It's Stacey.'

'Stacey who?'

'Arron's sister, have you heard?'

'Oh my god, yer I just saw the news, I'm so sorry.'

'Can we link up?'

'Yer of course man, when?'

'As soon as please.'

'In the morning if that any good to ya?'

'How's about 11, is that kool?'

'Looking forward to seeing you, I'll let you go. See you soon.'

'OK Stacey see you then.'

I end the call and look at Claire. 'Wot the fuck!'

'All this time, why now? I ain't his girl.'

'I dunno.' Claire shrugs her shoulders,

What more can go fucking wrong? Shit, now I have to go face Leona. We roll up and leave. I'm linking Claire's arm as were walking down the road, police sirens everywhere, I'm feeling a bit lean now, it's like I'm dreaming. Did Stacey just phone me? I don't understand, why do they wanna see me, it don't make no sense. Well I'll find out tomorrow, init.

We reach Veronica's. 'Where you two been?' she says, like she's a bit pissed off with us.

'Hi mum' I say, giving her a kiss on the cheek. 'I had to finish off my course work.'

'Oh you are a good girl.' She gives us both hugs and sends us upstairs

'I will bring you tea soon, all right?'

'Thanks mum' we say. We get to the bedroom door, Claire grabs my hand and gives me that look. I know what she's thinking, I nod, we go in. It's so nice to see her where she belongs.

Let her know

'You all right babe?' I say hugging her.

'Yer wot, no grapes na?' I kiss my teeth and we laugh.

'You all right babe?' Claire hugs her. (It's sad we nearly lost her.)

'Wot you two been up to?' She feels like she's missed so much!

'Do you remember Stacey?' I say.

'Stacey, not sure, the names rings a bell, who is it?'

'Arron's sister'?

'Why, what's happened to her?'

'Na nuffin, it's Arron.'

'Wot is he still troubling you, what wrong with him? He made his bed. Jen you ain't going back there are you, Claire man help me out.'

'Na it's not like that Leona' said Claire.

'Wot's it like then Jen? He hurt you so much he ain't good enough for you babe.'

'He's dead Leona!'

'*Wot?*'

'Yer man, his face has been all over the news and shit, then Stacey phones me wanting me to go round to hers in the morning.'

'Fucking hell Jen, wot happened?'

'Dunno. What about you Leona, how are you doll?'

'OK' she says.

'Any news?'

'As far as I know he's going up for bail. My solicitor said he could walk away from this. His story is airtight. Apparently he was beaten badly. They got pictures and everything, I don't know how he done it.'

She's all emotional. I give her a hug.

'Don't babe, it's gonna get sorted' I'm telling her.

'Yer, but if he walks that means my life ain't worth nuffin.'

I wipe the tears from her face. 'Worthless blood you na! Where's your phone?'

'Ere' she says and goes under her pillow.

'Why's it off babe?'

'I just can't deal with anything, Jen.'

'Wot, can I hold this?'

'Why?'

'Don't worry babe' I says. 'I'm gonna sort it, yer.'

'Take it then' she says.

'I've got a spare at home I'll bring it for you.'

The door opens, it's V with the tea and cake. We sit chatting about old times. I don't need to ask her anything, I've got it all in my pocket. That worked out well. She's asking me about Maggie. Next time Leona, too much is goin on with her, I can see she's getting tired.

'We're gonna make a move babe so you can rest.'

'When am I going to see you guys?'

'I'll pass in the morning while you go to check Stacey' said Claire.

'Then you can meet me back here, yer? Is that OK Leona?'

'Yer! Love you guys man.' She was happy to see us.

'Love you too babe.' We all have a cuddle, you know how girls stay.

'Do you want me to shut the light?' I say.

'Yes please babe, nite hun.'

We go downstairs and say our goodbyes. Veronica walks us to the door.

'We're coming tomorrow.'

'Yes that wot she need, you girls around her' she says. We kiss her

58

and leave. We end up at Claire's.

'So what's tomorrow about?' she asks.

'I really don't know why they're even phoning me, to tell you the truth. It might just be cos you was with him. I dunno man it don't ring right, why now? I haven't seen them for like 2 plus years.'

'Yer, that don't sound right' she said.

'You gonna be all right going by yourself?'

'Yer, it just doesn't make sense but we'll see, init.'

'Anyway, changing the subject, wot's on the phone?' Claire asks. I turn it on and go into contacts and scroll down. Yep, there he is. I tap his number in my phone, I'll keep that for next time. Let's look in the photos. As we're looking there's nuff of all of us.

'Go back Claire, that guy with Leona, what do you think?'

'Na man, I don't think so Jen.'

Claire's going through them while I'm making tea.

'Jen come look, I think you're right man, look that this' she says.

'Let me just finish making the tea, one minute babe.' I walk in.

'Look Jen, there's nuff in here.' I sit down next to her and she gives me the phone, I'm looking at this waste man. I know this guy, well not know him, but seen him somewhere, not sure where though.

'Does he ring any bells with you Claire? have a good look fam.'

'You saying that yer? Hold on, that's fucking what's his name.'

'Marcus' I say.

'Na I know him as... fuck, shit it's gone, na Penny that's fuckin Penny! Blood broke ass piece of shit man, he's a fucking wanker Jen. You know him man, remember that gal long time ago at the bus stop?'

'No?'

'Yer star, her man was hittin her, there was blood all over her! We beat him up remember, we left him spark out on the floor, she was cussing us to leave him.'

'Yes man crackheads, so wot the fuck was Leona doing with him?'

'You know how it is Jen, love is blind sometimes.'

'Yer but fucking hell, look at him man, blind for true.'

'So wot now?' Claire says.

'I can't slip up, you know wot I'm sayin init?'

'Trust me Jen, I don't chat nuffin to no one, not even Kriss, even if things come on top I don't know anything and you was ere anyway babe, if you do this I've got your back yer?' And she hugs me, there are no words for it but I love this girl.

'Wot we need to do is, yer, plan a nite in, know wot we're eating at wot time, what we're watching and at wot time to cover all grounds, wot do you think Claire?'

'Yer I like the way you're thinking Jen, you're really on this thing init.'

'If there's one thing I've learned, if you do summit do it right, go in with your eyes open and your wits about you at all times.'

'You ain't easy Jen.'

'You're damn right, if you let someone take the piss with you, then it leaves it open for other people to try walk all over ya, get me? Them days are over, trust, an I'm gonna make it clear to certain mans, yer! That the girls on the ends ain't having it.'

'Claire babe, I have to go get some sleep.'

'Stay Jen.'

'Na, I can't, I gotta go link Stacey in the morning init.'

I put my coat on give her a hug an on my way I go. It's so quiet out here, I'm thinking to myself. I play some music on my phone and before I know it I'm at home. I grab my pillow and my furry throw and make up a bed on the sofa, make tea, roll up, put the telly on, get stoned and fall asleep.

I don't wanna know

I wake up around 4 am, turn the telly off and go and jump in my bed. It feels so nice to just stretch out and find that one spot when you feel like your floating drifting off. I feel so relaxed and sleepy, my hair's in my face but I don't wanna move so I just leave it and sleep. I get up around 9.30 and just lounge about listening to the radio.

I've been thinking about Arron. It's sad man, he was only 22 and he was a nice guy even though he hurt me back then, we had something. He was my first love, I would have done anything for him once. When I found out wot he had done it hurt.

I cut everyone off. Thinking back, my heart's racing, I found out I was in the same boat as her. I didn't say anything to him, I just wanted him as far away from me as possible. He never knew and now he never will, I couldn't stay with him.

I remember the last time we was together, I could tell he had been somewhere else. He was a bit rough with me, that's not us, that's not how we was with each other. I lost the plot when I found out I was up the duff. I wasn't myself, I got a bit sick and ended up gettin rid. That was the worst day of my life. The state I was in I couldn't have had a baby, it wouldn't have been fair on no one. I wasn't in the right frame of mind, I couldn't even look after myself. I was messed up man.

As soon as I done it I knew it was the wrong thing but it was too late. My baby was gone, I killed it, and now every day I think about what I done and I hate myself for it. I don't deserve happiness, that's why I keep everyone at arm's length.

I get washed and dressed, roll up, I need it before I go. Wot if the girl is there? I don't need all this. I look at the time, it's 10.30 am. I'll have to leave soon, well when I finish smoking, I can't go there straight (I mean I need to be mash up for them people). Whatever they've got to say I'm gonna take it with a pinch of salt and get out of there.

They live at the back of Brixton down near the market. I leave and jump on the bus and get off at Brixton police station and walk through Popes Lane on to Electric Avenue, walk down and chuck a left. I can see the flats ain't been down here for time, I cross the road. We used to get nuff joke down ere, always doing summit, usually bad, but we was young, and yer, I know that's no excuse for bad behaviour, but this is where it all began for me. It just feels a bit weird after all this time.

I find the house, it still looks the same. I ring the bell and the door opens.

'Hello Jen.'

'Hiya Stacey, long time no see.'

'Come in' she says. As I go in I say to her 'Not bein' funny or anything, wot's going on?'

'Come sit down Jen, I need to talk to you.'

We go and sit in the front room. The house is really quiet.

'It's good to see you though' she says.

'Yer, you too. Wot happened with Arron, Stacey? Wot's all this about?'

'Do you want a drink or something?'

'Na I'm OK. Just say wotever it is, Stacey.'

'All right then, when all that stuff happened with you and Arron?'

'Yer, why you bringing that up?'

'Well give me a minute and I'll tell ya. That girl Lisa said she was pregnant for Arron. It turns out it's not his son after all.'

'Wot you talking about Stace, you're not making any sense. He told me the baby was his.'

'Yes I know Jen, we all thought he was, up to like maybe about 3 months ago.'

'So wot you telling me?'

'Someone told him he wasn't the baby's dad and he confronted her. She said she weren't sure who it was and that she wanted it to be him, so they done a DNA test and it turned out he weren't, it was the other guy. So that could mean anyone? He was so upset he started drinking hard, snorting coke, acting dumb. He never forgave himself for hurting you and all for nothing. He tried to stay and sort things out, we could all see he wasn't happy. Everything went wrong for them. You can't build a life on lies can you? Then it all started. He would go out looking for trouble, and he found it.'

Tears fill up in my eyes, I can't stop myself. We're both crying, holding each other.

'He went out angry as always, he was going up west end to one club, the Path. Do you know it?'

'Na.'

'There was a bit of trouble, a fight broke out. Arron got stabbed straight through his heart, gone just like that. I've always tried to help him but he just didn't care about nothing any more. The reason I asked you to come is to let you know my brother loved you so much. After wot happened I never saw him smile again, it's like he lost something and he couldn't find it. I could see the hurt when he looked at me, I mean what more could I have done?'

'I know you were always there for him Stacey.'

'Jen, there's some things you might want.'

'Na Stacey I don't want them, I've got my memories thanks.'

'You sure? Go and have a look.'

'No let your mum have them.'

'Jen, you seem really calm.'

'Yer, I feel calm. I am sorry what happened to Arron and yer, I did love him once, but a lot's gone on since then. Where's your mum, how is she?'

'She staying with Auntie Pat for a while.'

'Give her my love, yer?'

'I will do.'

'So do they know who done it?'

'They've arrested two men, but they think there's a third, they have some CCTV footage they're going through.'

'I hope it's clear and they can make out wot happened.' I say. 'Stacey I really have to go, I'm sorry.'

'Na, don't be, I'm so glad you came, Jen. Will you come to the funeral, Mum would love to see you?'

'Yer of course, you've got my number, bell me and let me know.' She walks me to the door, we say bye and I head home.

Everything she said is running through my head. I know it sounds harsh but the fact of the matter is he did cheat on me, baby or no baby, and yer things do happen an it's up to the persons involved wot they do an how they deal with it. I decided to let him go, I couldn't stay with that.

I get home. I was meant to go round to Leona's. I will get there, but not just yet. I don't feel hurt or nuffin, I just wanna see Kriss, I miss him so much.

I sit down and smoke a joint. Wow I think to myself, that's how some girls go on, lie and cheat to get wot they want, but not all of us are like that. I want to be an equal 50/50 in everything, no secrets, up front at all times. I'm not one of them girls who see a guy for what he's got, and he could have nothing, but be the nicest person, that would do me.

Kriss on the other hand has everything money can buy. I don't see that though. I never thought I would ever find someone like him. When I was young I used to think about when I was older would I get married and settle down. I used to try and picture his face but never could, but I knew wot kinda person he had to be. When I look at Kriss he's so beautiful and he's the nicest person I know apart from my family.

I'm feeling a bit mash up, better make my way over to the girls. I roll up a joint for the walk, grab the phone for Leona an leave, I feel drained.

I finally get there, it feels like I been walking for ages. I knock the door, Claire answers it.

'Wot took you that long babe?'

'Na, I had to go home for a bit.'

'You all right Jen?'

'I should be asking you that, babe. How you feeling today?'

'A lot better, how did it go?'

'Fine, it was something and nothing really. Let's not talk about it right now. Where's your mum?'

'She went out about an hour ago, bingo init. You look a bit mash up Jen.'

'Yer, I was smoking a joint on the way here.'

'You got any left?'

'Yep, you can roll it for yourself though, I'm going in the garden to finish this, is that kool?'

'Go for it babe, I'll just roll this, then I'm coming.'

'Wot about me?' says Claire.

'The things are there babe, you dunno, you don't have to ask.' I have to walk through the kitchen to get to the garden. Claire follows me.

'Leona, will you roll it for me?' Claire's so lazy.

'Yer, kool hun.'

'Wot happened Jen, you OK?'

'Yer, I'll tell you later.'

We're in the garden, they got one of them swing chairs. It's lovely out here. There's a water feature, it looks like the waters running from nowhere. It's wicked. We sit chatting. Leona says she hasn't seen Shelly.

'It coz she feels away' I say. Sometimes I should try an hold my lip, but fuck it she needs to know.

'Wot do you mean Jen?'

'Well, she knew about you. She said something weren't right and she still said nuffin, so she feels a bit to blame.'

'Na it's not like that. I asked her not to say anything, so I've only got myself to blame.'

'Wot na babe, she should have told us still, we could have done summit init.'

'I know, I feel so stupid' she said.

'Don't man, we all do things we're not proud of.'

'Things happen for a reason, as long as we learn from them, but wot you did was fucking dangerous You must have known it weren't right.'

'Yer I did, but I thought I could handle it.' She starts crying.

'I've caused so much trouble haven't I?' she says wiping her eyes.

'No way' says Claire. 'The main thing is that you're OK.'

I give her a hug and we go into the house and make some tea and put the radio on. I can see summit's on Leona's mind.

'Wot's up babe?'

'He's up in court tomorrow.' With that I can hear the key in the door. Veronica's back. 'Shhhhh don't say anything.'

'OK' I say.

The shit's hittin the fan

Veronica walks in, we say hello.

'You girls hungry?' she always thinks of others.

'Yer' we say.

She goes into the kitchen, she's in there a little while. Leona leans over.

'He's gonna get off with it. My solicitor phoned me.'

'Wot?'

'That it's not looking good. It's really his word against mine, and he's got a good case so it could be thrown out.'

'Don't worry' I say. 'Wotever way it's all gonna be all right.'

Veronica brings in chicken and rice for all of us. 'Mmmm thanks mum' says Leona, and we tuck in. This is the first proper meal I've had since my mum and that went to Bristol. Claire's use to takeaways, that's wot we call her, the take-out queen. She's got all the menus down, she's got them on speed dial.

It's a bit spicy for me so I just eat the rice and salad. Still nice though. We finish up and I go to wash up the plates.

'Leave that Jen, it will give me something to do later.'

'Na you're all right it's kool, do you want tea?'

'Yes please' she says. I finish the washing up and make V a cuppa and take it through to her. 'Thank you' she says.

'It's OK, any time' I say. Us girls go upstairs.

'So you gonna let us know the outcome?'

'Yer, I'll get a call, then I'll tell you.'

'We're gonna leave soon, babe I'm tired, I need to go to my bed and have a good night's sleep. Do you wanna stay at mine Claire?'

'Yer go on then, yours is nearer than mine.'

'Oh thanks.' Wotever.

'Na I didn't mean it like that.'

We're all laughing, it's nice to see Leona happy.

'We're gonna go now babe.'

'OK I'll speak to you tomorrow.'

We go to say bye to V and bless her she's asleep. There's a throw on the sofa so I put it over her and we leave, shutting the door softly. We're walking up the road.

'So you gonna tell me wot happened Jen?'

'Boy, I don't even know where to start. Well, Arron has a baby but it turns out that it's not his.'

'Fuck' said Claire.

'Its bad, init. They found out a few months ago.'

'Wot you saying man?'

'I know, but anyway, after that he lost the plot drinking, taking hard drugs, going out looking for trouble, fighting. Not very nice by all accounts. The night it happened Stacey said he went out angry. Went to one club up west, got into a fight and got stabbed one time through the heart.'

'Shut up!'

'Swear down.'

'That's wot she wanted to tell you.'

'Na, she said he loved me and he hurt me for nothing. He was trying to do the best by his kid, but it weren't his.'

'How do you feel about that Jen?'

'Nuffin. Yes it's really sad he's dead, but he knew when he slept with her if I ever found out that would be it, so no I don't feel no way.'

'Didn't you want to try work things out with him?'

'For wot? The trust had gone, simple as that.'

We get to mine, Claire has a coffee and we chat some more.

'I'm gonna go to the funeral' I tell her.

'Why?'

'Cos the family asked me and out of respect, I'll go to the church and then I'll leave.'

'When is it?'

'I don't know, Stacey gonna bell me'

I roll a joint and pass Claire the rizla. We smoked so much I felt sick. Claire's on the sofa leaning so far over she might as well be lying down, she gives me so much joke! Don't know what I would do without her.

Then she just comes out with, 'Kriss can't wait to see you. he phones me every day Jen, he says he's checking up on me but we always end up taking about you.'

'That's nice, really nice' I say.

'So you and my brother yer, I'm happy, I never like his girls none of them.' She kinda sits up and looks at me. 'But Jen I love ya, you know.'

'Shut up Claire.' I say.

'Na, swear down babe, you're good for him. When he's with you he's happy. The way he talks about you, if a man spoke about me like that, wow! that would be something else.'

She's chatting mash up talk now, she ain't even making sense, but I hope it's true cos that's how I feel about him too. I go to say summit to Claire, she's lick out. When Arron done what he did I couldn't be bothered with guys no more, they were a waste of space, a bunch of wankers. Not all but most of them. Now Kriss has opened my eyes to how things should be, I'm a lucky girl. I hope it's for real.

My blanket's still on the sofa, I put it over her and go jump in my bed. The room's spinning a bit so I roll over and lie on my front. The room slows down a bit but it's still moving. I fall asleep.

We just kids really

It's morning, I go into the front room, Claire's hanging off the sofa half on half off. I help her back on and go put the kettle on, I look at the time, 8.30. I give my mum a ring.

'Hello my darling' she says.

'Hi mum you all right?'

'Yes I'm fine, wot you been up to jennie?'

'My course work's all done.'

'Oh good girl, how was it?'

'OK.'

'How's everyone?'

'Well' she says.

'We all went out to the balloon festival yesterday, you would have liked it, when we got back you know, Anne's dog has puppies?'

'Yer?'

'Well they ripped the wallpaper and peed and poohed everywhere.'

'Oh no!' I start laughing.

'It's not funny Jennie, it was a bloody state.'

'I've got to go now mum, my credit gonna run out, love you, say hi to everyone for me.'

'I will do honey.'

'Bye mum.'

'Bye, love you too' and she hangs up.

I make my tea and go and sit down, Today's the day, I think everything's caught up with me. I go back to my room and lie down and before I know I'm sleeping. I have a weird dream that Arron's running through the streets shouting my name but I couldn't find him, wot the fuck was that about?

I get up and jump in the shower, that woke me up nicely, I go into the front room, Claire's still sleeping, I go over to her and ask her she wants tea.

'Can I have coffee babe?'

'Yer, kool.' I go to the kitchen and remember we're out of milk.

'I have to go shop.'

'For wot?'

'Milk.'

'Na babe, I'll have it black, I need it.'

I have a hot chocolate, it don't need milk. I can't drink coffee, it sends me to sleep, weird or what?

'So wot you on today Jen?'

'Nothing babe, one of them days you know, when you just wanna be in your house.'

'Yer babe, and wot about Leona?'

'She'll bell me when she knows, I'll come get ya.'

'I'm going home to bed.'

'All right babe later.' I jump on the sofa and get comfy. Shelly's on my mind, I'm gonna go check her. I send her a text, *Hiya hun can we link up today x.* Get one back, *Hi babe where are you x*

At home x

Kool I'm gonna come to you x

Just reach when you're ready x

xxx

I iron summit to put on, get ready and wait for her to come, after a while the door goes, I go an open it.

'You all right Jen?' she says with open arms.

'Wot's good babe?' I give her a hug.

'Come man its cold! Get in here.' We go inside.

'So how's everything babe?' she says.

'So much has been going on.'

'Like wot Jen? You kool though, yer?'

'Yer I'm fine, have you heard about Arron?'

'No, what's he done now babe?'

'His sister phoned me the other day.'

'Why though?'

'He's dead.'

'Don't lie! Wot happened?'

I tell her wot Stacey told me, she burst into tears, I give her a cuddle. I know she had nuff love for him as we all did back then, but things change. I really want to phone Kriss but I can't, it's like something stopping me, I don't know what's wrong with me. I pull away from her.

'You all right?'

'Wot happen Jen?' she says, sobbing. 'Wot's fucking wrong with people, why they had to take it so far?'

That's how it is on road now days, all you have to do is look at someone the wrong way that could be it, you know what I mean? You never think it's gonna happen to you but shit does and we have to deal with it the best we can. But life goes on and we have to do what we have to do for ourselves. There's a lot of fuckry people out there.

'Where you been anyway, it's come like you fell off the planet?'

'It's not even like that Jen, I just felt away with this Leona thing.'

'Why man?'

'Cos I never said anything init, and look wot happened, but I know now, trust me it won't happen again.'

'She really wants to see you.'

'But I let her down.'

'She doesn't see it that way, she trusts you man!'

'She asked you not to say anything and you didn't, she just don't understand why you ain't been to check her.'

'So wot then?' I'm waiting for her to say summit.

'I'll go round, will you come with me Jen?'

'Na babe you gotta do this on your own, she's at home I think, you should go round, she needs you today.'

'Why, what's going on?'

'Go round and find out, ask Leona.'

'All right I'm going. Love you.'

'Love you too babe' and I walk her to the door.

'Kiss her for me, yer?'

'I will do, see you soon.'

'Make sure I wanna hear about what's going on with you next time though, go see Leona.'

I send Kriss a text, *thinking about you xx* short and sweet. I pop over to the shop.

'Hi Ali.'

'Afternoon Jennie, how are you today, and your mum?'

'I'm good, the family's still away.'

'And you, everyone back now?'

'No they're coming back home Sunday.'

'That's nice I say.'

'Well I enjoy myself when they gone, but you know they say all good things have to end.' We're laughing. I grab milk and bread, pay and leave.

'Bye Ali.'

'See you Jennie.'

I get back home and make myself tea and toast. My phone's beeping, I smile, a message from Kriss. *I can't wait to get home to see you darling, miss you more everyday xxx*

Wot more could I want? I know he's out there working hard, it's wot he does, but it don't stop me from worrying. He's so smart, I'm not even kidding, he could do anything go anywhere, everyone likes him I've never heard anybody diss him, but the line of work he's in, on road, yes I worry. I would never ask him to stop, that's his thing, how he makes his living, to put a roof over him and his sisters head. I know people look down on people who sell drugs, but if there's a need for it why not? Shops sell alcohol, it's the same thing, well worse I think.

The phone rings, its Leona, crying.

'He got off, they threw it out.'

'Wot? Calm down.' I'm not really hearing wot she's saying.

'They got all the paperwork and some background report that showed he's a crackhead and they believed his accounts of wot happened.'

'I'm coming round, OK? I'll be there now, I'm leaving.'

I cut the phone, brush my hair, jacket on and go, walking up the road thinking fucking hell here we go this is it shit, hoped it wouldn't come to this but it has and I have to deal with it. I have to stay calm and in control, can't let them know wot's really going on.

I arrive at the house, I'm outside, not really sure what I'm walking into. I take a few minutes to collect my thoughts, here we go. I knock the door and Veronica opens it. I can see she's been crying. I just put my arms around her and hold her, she holds me so tight bless her, little does she know, I'm gonna sort this shit out! I mean wot can I say really? Everyone's hurting, the vibe in the house is horrible. V takes me by the hand through to the kitchen.

'Wot's going on Jen? I just don't understand. The law let Leona down, they told us that horrible man was going to go away for a long time and that he won't be able to hurt anyone else, but they just let him go just like that, that's just sending out a message that you can do anything you want and get away with it.'

'I know V, I can't believe it.'

'Why Jennie? We're not bad people. My one and only child nearly dead, but that's all right! How dare they?'

With that she hands me a cup of tea and sends me upstairs. As I'm walkin up the passage I pop my head round the front room door, say hello to everyone and head upstairs. I can hear talking and I open the door. Sonia, Shelly and Leona all sitting on the bed. I can see Shelly's been crying. I go an hug Leona, she's trying to tell me wot happened but nothing coming out right. She's just kept on saying it's her own fault, maybe she deserved it.

'Don't man' I say.

'But Jen!'

'I don't even want to hear it Leona, at the end of the day you're here alive and kicking, you're gonna be fine, anything is gonna be OK.'

Inside I'm fuming, I'm so fucking angry. If he was in front of me I would rip his fucking head off, that's the way I feel. I walk around the side of the bed and give Sonia a hug

'How you been babe?' I ask her.

'Good babe, you? How's college?'

'Really good, I'm so enjoying it.'

'That's nice to hear Jen. I always knew you was going places.'

'Ah thanks Sonia that's nice, but yer, I'm tryin a ting still.'

'So you two, have you sorted out your thing?'

'Yer, we're kool, always' Leona says.

Here we go

Shelly was like 'I've got something to say while we're all here.'

'Wot's up babe?'

'Well I'm not sure, but I don't know.'

'Wot's wrong babe? Remember we don't hide nothing no more, we're all up front from this day onwards. So wot is it?'

She just comes out with it. 'I think I'm pregnant.'

'Wot!' Leona shouts out. I see Sonia smile.

'Have you done a test babe?' I say.

'Na I don't need one, I just know.'

'We gotta go get one now' I say,

'I've got one in my bag' she says.

'When you texted me this morning Jen, it was like a sign, I swear.'

'So wot you saying? Go and pee on it now man.'

'I can't, I'm scared.'

'Why babe, you don't want it?'

'Na I do, but well what about, ah man I can't do this' she says.

'Wot's wrong? Are you scared of wot the baby father is gonna say? Who is the dad?'

She looks right at me and says 'It's Jason'.

'Jason who? Do we know him?'

'Jason, my holiday thing.'

'Oh that Jason. Has you talked to him yet?'

'Na, I need to know first.'

'Well we can't do nuffin about that right now until we know, so go an take the test, we're all here for you.'

She grabs her bag and goes into the toilet, it feels like she's been gone ages. None of us are saying anything, you could hear a pin drop.

The door opens!

'Well?' I say. Shelly just nods.

Leona's all happy. 'We're gonna have a baby! You are gonna have it aren't you?' she asks. 'Shelly, you all right?'

'Jen, wot am I gonna do?' She don't look too happy.

'What do you mean?' I go and sit next to her.

'Jason's married.'

'Wot!' We all look at each other. 'Wot do you mean married?'

'I didn't know when I was in Jamaica. I found out when I got home.'

'Hold on a minute, back up' I say.

'I know Jen, and now look. Wot a mess, I'm in shit!'

'You still have to let him know though.'

Little shit, that's wot I'm talking about, them waste man outta road, they got their gal, wife wotever, but still find themselves somewhere else, wot's that all about? Why can't a man be happy with just one girl? Fucking hell is that too much to ask?

'So wot did he say? How did you find out babe?'

'He phoned me and said he's got a wife and young kids, so he can't afford the flight here and could I pay.'

'Are you joking? Really? So wot, she knows about you?'

'I don't know Jen, I was with him all the time out there, it didn't even cross my mind. I thought he was single and that's the way he came across.'

'Why didn't you ask him before freeing up yourself? Wot's wrong with you?'

'I don't know.'

'Wot do you mean for fuck sake? Come on, we're all big now, we should all know better. Now look, you're up the duff with some fucking waste man, Leona put a wanker in her life and he fucked her up, Maggie's a fucking druggie, and Sonia wot have you got to tell us? Cos fuck there's gotta be something!' I don't know what happened, I just lost it for a minute.

'Na I'm kool Jen' she said, with her head down.

'Everybody in here means so much to me, all of you. I love you guys! Right Shelly, wot you gonna do babe?'

'I don't know Jen, how I can have a kid?'

'We're all here for you, we'll help you, think about it long and hard yer, and then you let us know.'

'Leona, I understand wot happened to you today, we all do, and to let you know nothing like that will ever happen again trust! But you have to be up front with us all the time. Remember wot goes around comes around. He will get his, yer? Sonia I love you, we all do, it just feels like we're all growing apart. We need to pull back together, be there for each other always no matter wot. I promise you all that everything will be OK I know it don't seem that way now, but it will in time.'

We have a right laugh about the good old days; well I say that, but we're still young ourselves!

'Right girls, I'm a love ya and leave ya.'

'Where you off Jen?'

'Gotta see a man about a dog' I say with a wink, say my byes and leave.

Never before

I go home and just flop in the chair, I've got a blinding headache and go and look for some pills. I take two an go an lie down for a bit. I feel sick with everything, why can't I have just one good day where nothing bad happens and everything is good?

I get up and go to the kitchen an grab a glass of water, then I go back to bed My head's banging, I'm just gonna lay here until i drift off.

I wake up, its dark outside, I look over - fuck, it's 3 am. I get up and go and sit down in the front room. I thought it would be nice here without the rest of my family but I've never missed them so much.

My phone rings (thinking to myself who could it be at this hour), so many things are running through my head. I answer it.

'Hello who that?'

'It's me babe.' Kriss.

'Hello.'

'Wot you doing up this early Jen?'

'Weren't feeling too good last night, now I can't sleep. When you coming home?'

'I'm outside' he said. 'you gonna let me in?'

'Shut up, for true?'

'Come see.'

I go to open it. I hope he is here. I unlock the door and pull it. For true there's Kriss, flowers and all.

'Hello darling, come here.'

I walk towards him and fling my arms round him and hold him so tight,

'I've missed you babe' he said. 'who's in?'

'No one.'

'Come on then.' Hand in hand we go in and he turns the key in the door. I'm not feeling nothing, not scared, worried or anything, just happy, really happy he's here.

'I thought you weren't back for a few days?'

'Yer, Claire phoned me and told me wot happened so here I am. How are you babe? These are for you darling.'

'For me? It feels a bit funny, no one's ever bought me flowers. They're gorgeous' I say, putting them in water. 'I'm all right. Things just seem to be getting worse, but I've realised wot's important to me. Well it's you, it's all about you.'

He smiles. 'So wot are you saying Jen?'

'I'm saying I want you in my life, but things are tough right now, I got something to sort out.'

He looks at me. 'Wot's that then?'

I don't wanna hide anything from him any more. 'Can we sit a minute?'

'Wot's going on Jen?'

'It's this thing with Leona, it's all gone pear shaped, the case got thrown out.'

'You're joking! Wot happened?'

'It's a long ting but I'm gonna sort it out.'

'Na Jen, I'll get it sorted for ya.'

'Kriss, I told you back when it happened I can sort this for myself, you can't get involved. I won't let you.'

'So wot you sayin then?'

'That's why I haven't let anything happen between us. I can't until all this is out the way, but you most probably won't want anything to do with me now.'

He walks over to me,

'Jen, I need to tell you something, that's why I'm here. I know you better than you know yourself. We've grown together. Wotever it is, I ain't gonna love you no less.'

'Love?'

'Yer I do, I love ya, I have done for the longest time.'

'You love me Kriss?' I'm smiling like a fool.

'Yer. You know I can't let you do this on your own, you need help.'

'You can't! You don't understand, this is something I have to do by myself.'

I don't know what I'm feeling. I'm happy when I see him, I can't wait to be with him, when he went away I don't ever want to feel like that again, it was horrible.

Too much too soon

'Kriss I really want us to work, I'm just scared.'

'Why darling?'

'Maybe the way I feel for you is too much. Now look, it's all come at the wrong time.'

'Na' he said. 'This is the right time, it's our time. Just give it a chance.'

I look at him, he's everything I've ever wanted. I kiss him, it feels so right, his arms around me holding me, he's kissing my neck (I hope he understands).

'I want this' I say 'I want you.'

'Are you sure babe, are you?' he says kissing me.

He starts to undo my top. I pull away, not sure why though.

'Wot's wrong babe?' he says.

'Nuffin.'

'Talk to me, wotever it is.'

'Just don't want to get hurt, Kriss for me to give myself, that's deep. I'm feeling a bit scared now.'

'Of wot, me babe?'

'Na, the situation.'

'I would never hurt you Jen, I've been waiting for this for you for the longest time, I wouldn't mess it up.'

'Yer I know, I'm sorry.'

'Na man sorry for wot for being you? I wouldn't have it no other way, it's kool. When you're ready. You gonna make me a drink babe, wot would you like?'

He looks at me and bites his lip,

'You're so rude' I say, he laughs.

'Could I have something cold?'

'Juice or summit strong?'

'Juice babe.' I go and pour him a coke, he's rolling up.

'Come sit with me' he says.

On the sofa, one minute we're cracking joke an smoking, then we're kissing. Things are getting a bit steamy in here (I haven't been with anyone since Arron, it's been a long time.) I love kissing Kriss, he so soft and gentle, his body's to die for. My hands are all over him, I can't help myself.

'Let's go to my room.'

'You sure?' he says.

'See how it goes.' I don't know what happened to me, so we're in my room. I roll a joint, he's walking round looking at all my things.

'You know Jen, I've never been in your bedroom.'

'No one has, count yourself lucky.' We laugh.

'Wot no one?'

'No one.'

He comes and sits next to me and takes my spliff and rests it in the ashtray. Then he starts kissing me, it feels so nice. He takes off his top. Fucking hell! I'm laying down, he's on his knees. He leans to me and starts to undo my top and I sit up so I can get my arms out of the sleeves as we're still kissing. Now we're both in our undies. The lights on, so I get to have a good look at him. His body's so trim he could be a model. His tattoos are really nice, I've got a few myself.

Now it's skin to skin, he's so soft and smells so good I can't help it. I roll him over, now I'm on top, kissing him, but the kissing's changed, it feels more meaningful, more intense. The way he's touching me now he makes me feel it's magic.

'Are you OK babe? Do you want to stop?'

'No' I say, kissing him. We strip right down to nuffin, oh my god is this really happening?

'I'm gonna take it slow' he whispers. He starts kissing my body. It feels, there's no words how he was making me feel, he's kissing my face and looks at me.

'You're so beautiful. Are you ready?' I nod my head, he puts his hand down to find where he's going.

'You OK babe?'

'Yer I'm kool.'

He kisses me and at the same time starts moving slowly so now he's there. We're together moving as one. The way he is with me I've never felt nuffin like it. 'Slowly' I say, I can feel every movement. I've liked him for so long, now he's in my bed, we're all sweaty, slipping and sliding. Slowly does it, I don't wanna make him come too quick, I'm enjoying myself.

Watch him. 'Oh babe yer!'

I have a little giggle to myself, people are funny when they're having sex. He lifts my legs on to his shoulders, kissing them, running his hand over me, slowly moving deeper, looking straight at me saying how good I feel and givin it to me. The boy can fuck. Wot makes it even better, we came at the same time, it's powerful.

He kisses me and asks if it was OK. It's all I thought it would be and more.

'That's it now, you and me' he says. It sounds so right. This is where I want to be. He's amazing!

We just lie there in each other's arms.

'Wot's your dad gonna say about us?'

'He knows something's going on. He's kool, as long as I'm happy he's happy. My mum's gonna love it, you know she likes you. Over the years I've mentioned it she knows how much I check for you.'

'Is it?' he said. 'Wot you been saying then?'

'You'll find out all in good time.'

'I've wanted this for so long Jen, now I've got you there's no letting go' he says, kissing me.

'I don't know how we've managed to keep away from each other for so long.'

'Well you were young and my sister's friend.'

'And now?'

'I just can't do it any more living a lie, hiding my feelings. You're the only girl that I truly wanted. The rest of them were just there hanging on, but that's not what I want, that's not who I am.'

'Oh babe!'

'Na its true, you can ask Claire. I've always asked after you, making sure you're all right without you knowing. Now I want you to know, I'm not one of them men out there telling you one thing and doing another. Cards on the table I want you like never before darling. When I was away I weren't no good to anyone, I was itching to get back to London to see ya, I can tell you now and feel no way. Wot you thinking Jen?'

'That I feel like the luckiest girl right now. But why me?'

'Cos you're up front, you're caring, you're funny, you make me laugh, you're beautiful - look at you! Lucky, that's me babe. You've got your head screwed on right, you know what you want and you work hard to get it, and that's what I fell for. And you, what do you see in me?'

'I trust you with my life Kriss, and that's the truth. Remember before you went away we went for that drive and you took me to the café where you used to go with your mum?'

'Yer' he said, kissing me.

We belong

'And then we went on to your old house. You showed me something that night, I think that's when I fell for you. You told me stuff, deep things I'm sure you wouldn't have shared with no one else cos I know you're not like that. We shared a room that night and I told you I weren't ready and you respected me. I feel safe with you.'

'Say it then' he said.

'Say wot babe?'

'You know.'

I look at him, my heart's pumping so hard I can hear it. I kiss him softly and say

'I'm fallin in love with you.' He smiles and holds me tight.

'You've made me so happy' he says, squeezing me.

'One minute' I say. 'I need to use the bath room.'

I have a little wash and bring a flannel for Kriss. He's making tea wearing a towel. I'm watching him from the doorway. Is this for real, I ask myself? He's fucking hot, I can't take my eyes off him.

With that he turns round and walks towards me.

'I've made you tea babes, should we have it in bed?'

'Yer, come then.' It's like 7.30. 'I really need to sleep' I say.

'Do you want me to go?'

'Na babe, stay with me.'

We get in bed. It's a long time since I've share a bed with anyone. I fall asleep in Kriss's arms. I wake up and open my eyes.

'Morning babe' he says, kissing me.

'Morning darling, how you feeling? How did you sleep?'

'I haven't, I couldn't sleep knowing you was next to me.'

'Why?' I ask him.

'You're all I've wanted for so long. I can't believe my luck Jen.'

'But I could say the same. You need to rest babe. You were driving to all hours last night, then we stayed up late.' I kiss him. 'Now sleep. I'll be here when you wake up.'

'You're not going out are ya?'

'No babe, sleep now, yer?'

I go and run a bath, and just lie in it for a while thinking about last night and smiling to myself. Today's a good day, it's the first day of me and Kriss. I hope there's many more.

I'm out of the bath drying my hair. I pop my head round the bedroom door, he's fast asleep. I kiss him just to make sure he's really there. He stirs. 'Come' he says, holding out his hand.

I climb on to the bed; he puts his arm around me.

'You smell so good' he says, breathing deeply. He's moving his hand over my body, before I know it we were kissing. Our bodies are rubbing up against each other. Last night was sex, really good sex, but this morning we're making love, slowly touching, kissing, pleasing each other. All the way through he's asking me if I'm OK. I've never felt this feeling.

'Let go Jen, enjoy it.'

Oh my god, what the hell, I can't control myself.

'That's its babe.'

My breathing gets shallow, my body feels like fireworks. I let go.

'Oh yer' he says.

I close my eyes an it's like something takes over, I've never felt so much pleasure. We're still kissing for a while afterwards,

'Babe' he says. 'Fucking hell.' He's shaking his head.

'Did I do something wrong?'

'Na you're amazing, the way you feel.'

'Wot do you mean?'

'The way you make me feel, the way you feel. I don't know if I can keep my hands off ya.'

That's nice to hear. We have a cuddle and fall asleep. I had forgotten how much it takes out of ya. Sex that is.

I wake up to my phone ringing. I've got one of them ringtones from the 80s (don't stop the music), I love it. I don't want to wake Kriss up so I go and answer it in the other room. It's Shelly.

'Wot's up babe.'

'Jen, can I pass by you?'

'Yer come on then, I'll put the kettle on.'

'See you in like 10' she says.

I fling a tracky suit on, wondering what's happened now. I make my tea and set her cup, and wait. Before I know it I hear the gate open. I go an answer the door. I can see she looks worried.

'Wot's wrong babe? Come man.'

We go into the kitchen I make her tea, we sit down.

'You all right Shelly?'

'Did you mean wot you said the other day?' she asks.

'Wot you talking about, what I did I say?'

'That if I have the baby, we will all pull together. Did you mean it?'

'Of cos babe, we're all here for you. So you having, it yer?'

'Yes' she says.

'Have you told the rest of the girls?'

'Na not yet.'

'We'll get them all here tonight and let them know' I say. 'You hungry Shelly?'

'Yer, all the time.'

'Go and sit down and I'll make you summit.'

I can hear her from the front room. 'Who was ere last nite babe? Wot you been up to, and who gave you these flowers? They're lovely Jen.'

I walk in smiling. 'Wot man?' I say laughing.

'Who is it?'

She looks at me and puts her hand over her mouth. 'It's Kriss init' she says smiling. 'Is he ere?'

'Yer, he's in bed sleeping.'

'Oh my god Jen wot's going on with you two? Wot, you guys together now?'

'I hope so, it took long enough' I say. She's hugging me.

'I'm happy for you, he loves you man.'

'Yer I know he's does. He's sweet man.'

I go and plate up her food. It's just toast, beans, fried egg and mushrooms. I take it through to her.

'Here you go babe, hope it's OK.'

'Thanks Jen.'

'Should I text the girls about tonight?'

'Yer please babe' she says, scoffing her face.

I send the same text to everyone: *hi babe mine tonight about 7pm make sure you reach xx*

'So Shelly, have you had time to talk to Jason?'

'Na, I don't want him to know Jen.'

'Why not?'

'He's not the person I thought he was, he's nothing but a liar. I hate him. Lots of women do it by themselves and I'm no different. I've got my mum and you lot, Mark's gonna be an uncle, he'll think that's wicked.'

'Have you told your mum yet?'

'Na, I want to go doctors first. Will you come Jen?'

'When is your appointment?'

'4.30, sorry to just put it on you babe.'

'Na kool, I'll follow you. Wot's the time now?'

'3.45.'

'All right, let me just change my clothes. You can make me tea, seen as you draggin me out my house.'

'Sorry man.'

'Shut up Shelly, I'm joking, but I do want tea though.'

I go to my room for a minute, I forgot Kriss was in there until I saw him lying there, fucking hell I think to myself is he really mine for true? I'm changing my clothes and I hear a voice say 'Hello darling.' I turn round to see him smiling at me (I wish you could have seen it). He's got one of them sexy voices, it makes you want to rip your clothes off, but him as a package he's got it all. He really does look after himself, from his hair to his dress sense he's hot.

'Where you going babe?'

'Just got to pop to the doctor's.'

'Wot's wrong?'

'It's not me.'

As I get on the bed and kiss him, he puts his arms round me.

'Who then?'

'Shelly, she's pregnant.'

'Who's the dad?'

'Some waste man in Jamaica.'

'It's like that, yer' he says.

'Yer, but we're here for her.'

'You're so lovely, aren't you.'

'Kriss, you gonna be here when I get back?'

'Do you want me to be?'

'Yer of course. Just stay in bed.'

'Do you want anything before I go?'

'I'll do it babe, you go' he says, kissing me, he's very kissy touchy feely, I like it.

'I soon come, I grab my coat, we ready' I say. Shelly's like 'but I made your tea?'

I pick up the cup and take it through to Kriss. 'Thanks babe.'

'I won't be long.'

Making sure

We get to the doctors. I hate these places, they smell funny. We're sitting there not really knowing wot to say, so we say nuffin. She's scared and me more so, I don't know wot I'm doing, what to expect.

The monitor calls, 'Miss Shelly Chapman', she looks at me.

'Let's go' I say, we walk through.

'Do you want me to wait outside babe?'

'Na come with me.' She grabs my hand.

We knock the door, 'Come.' We go in.

'Hello I'm Dr Okkie. What can I do for you today?'

'Well' Shelly says, 'I've done a pregnancy test and it read positive.'

'OK' the doc replies. 'Let's do a test and take it from there.'

Shelly goes and has a pee and the doctor does the test.

'Well yes you're right, you are pregnant. What would you like to do?'

Shelly looks at me. 'Go on' I say.

'I want to keep it' she says.

'OK, congratulations. I'm gonna book you in at the antenatal clinic, so you'll get your appointment through the post. Is there anything else?'

'No thanks doc.'

We leave. 'Wot you gonna do now Shelly?'

'Go and tell my mum. I have to do it now.'

'Meet me back at mine, it's gonna be all right. See you later babe.'

Shelly goes off and I make my way home, I get in and call out for Kriss.

'I'm in the bathroom' he says. I open the door. 'Can I come in?'

'Come babe, wot happened?'

'Shelly having a baby. I can't believe it, she's gone home to tell her mum! I don't know wot she's gonna say.'

'Well she'll have to deal with it' Kriss says.

'Wot's that smell? Have you put something in the water?'

'Yer that bottle there, it's nice. I feel all relaxed.'

I laugh. 'This one?' I point to a blue bottle.

'Yer I like it. Why you laughing?'

'It's my mum's.'

'What's it for?'

'Well for one it's cream, and two it's for wrinkles! Did you even bother to read it?'

'Na, it was near the bath so I just thought it must go in there. My skin feels nice though, feel.'

'Didn't you wonder where the bubbles were?'

'Not really, I just jumped in.'

'You're so funny. You hungry babe?' I say smiling,

'Yer, starving. Do you wanna go out an grab something?'

'Yer kool. I don't mind making it for you.'

'Na, I wanna take you out.'

'But I haven't got long. The girls are coming for about 7.'

'That's fine, we'll be back by then.'

I like the way he says we, me and him. I feel so at ease with him, he's my Mr Wonderful. Swear down, he comes out of the bathroom looking good.

'You weren't wearing that last night was ya?'

'Na, I had clothes in the car. Should we go?'

'Yep.'

'Wot do you fancy?'

If only he knew wot I was thinking we wouldn't be going out, but a

92

man has to eat. We get in the car and drive off, we go to one Thai restaurant up Streatham, the food's so good here. Kriss orders, and I'm watching the time.

'Have you seen Claire?' I ask him.

'Na, I belled her earlier, she knows I'm back and at yours. She said she'll see us later.'

He holds my hand across the table and looks into my eyes.

'You've made me so happy you know, you're a beautiful person and I'm glad you're in my life.'

'Babes' I say. A tear runs down my cheek.

'Don't get upset.' he pulls his chair near and puts his arm around me. 'Come ere, Jen. Wot is it? I'm just glad we're finally together, I don't need to hide my feelings any more I can just be me, do ya know wot I mean? I always thought you didn't like me, well that's the impression you gave out.'

'That's just the way I am Kriss, unreadable. I'm not one of them people who wear their heart on their sleeve, better late than never.'

I eat a little, it's nice but too much for me. Kriss is like 'You not hungry babe?'

'I don't really eat out, certain foods hurt me.'

'Oh yer, sorry babe, do you wanna get something else?'

'No baby I'm kool.'

We finish up and leave.

'Can we stop off?' I'm saying. 'I need to pick up a few things for tonight.'

We park up and go in, Kriss has got the trolley. It's nice, we're like a proper couple. We grab some nibbles, a few bottles of pop, some wine, and we go to pay.

'I'll get this Jen.'

'No its OK.' Before I could get my money out Kriss had paid.

'You're so naughty' I say.

'Watch when I get you home, I'm gonna show you naughty' he says.

The checkout girl starts laughing. 'You lucky girl, is he your boyfriend?' I felt so proud to be able to say 'yes he is.'

He grabs my hand and we walk out to the car, he starts kissing me. I mean we're making out in the bloody car park, people are walking past and all sorts! I heard someone say 'Get in there, go on bruv'. We had a giggle and drove home.

Goin back home

On the way Kriss gets a call. He gets a bit pissed off with whoever he was talking to.

'I have to fly up the road. Are you kool to follow me babe?'

'Is it far?'

'Na, just Stockwell'

'Kool.'

It's on the way to mine anyway; he pulls up, uses his phone.

'I'm outside now' he's saying. The tone in his voice ain't joking. A minute or so later I see two men walking towards the car. Kriss says 'I soon come.'

He gets out the car. I can hear raised voices, my heart's going, I'm in two minds to get out myself, I'm trying to see wot's happening. Kriss has got hold of one of them. With that I see the one he's got hold of fall and hit the ground, hard. The other guy's got his arms out trying to calm Kriss down, well that's what I think from wot I can make out. The other guy goes and gets something and gives it to Kriss, a bag or summit, some more words are exchanged. Then Kriss heads back to the car. He doesn't really say nuffin about wot happened.

'So wot time is everyone getting to yours babe?'

He says it all calm, just like that, like nothing happened. I go along with it

'Sevenish' I say.

Seeing him like, that really turned me on. He's sexy when he's angry. Well he's sexy full stop.

'Is it kool for me to come and chill with you guys?'

'You don't have to ask, I want you to stay, I love it when you're around, it's nice.'

We get to mine and go in. Kriss helps me get everything ready for the girls, he's lovely like that. The bag he picked up from those guys goes straight under my bed.

'Wot's in there?' I say. I need to know.

'Money, is that all right? I don't really want to leave it in the car overnight.'

'Na its OK, as long as it's money and nuffin else.'

He comes over to me. 'I would never bring nuffin ere and that's no lie babe, never would I do you like that, trust.'

And I do trust him.

He makes tea. He loves it as much as I do. He rolls a joint and passes it to me to light. I wish them lot weren't coming but I'm sure they won't stay, Kriss is ere. I'm feeling a bit mash up.

'Where did you get this weed?' I ask him.

'Up north, it's nice init.' Well like anybody he buys a draw off his people, cos the money goes back in. Just cos it's his things don't mean shit! Money has to be made, so it would be bad practice to just smoke for free, then if all the mans done the same thing, do you know how much peas would be lost?

We're sitting on the sofa. I'm feeling really lean, right about now! I don't know wot came over me man. I climbed on Kriss's lap, I've wanted to do this all day. Kissing him is pure pleasure, I can't get enough. He picks me up and lays me down so gently. As we're getting into things, the door goes!

'Leave it' Kriss says. He's kissing and holding me.

I don't want to but I have to answer it. We fix up and I go an let them in.

'Hiya' I say, still trying to fix up. It's Shelly, Sonia, Leona and Claire all together. We all go through, everyone says hello. Kriss and Claire have a cuddle, they're having a little chat. I can see she happy with wotever's been said cos she comes over to me and chucks her arms around me and whispers in my ear.

'I'm so happy Jen. You two make a lovely couple.'

'Thanks babe.' That was nice of her, that's one thing, I don't want this to come between us!

'Wot's goin' on you guys?' Leona asks. She's too fast sometimes.

I smile, so does Kriss. I go sit on his lap and kiss him, they're like 'We knew it!' Now they're gonna start, so I turn round to them and say 'There's food and that in the kitchen, help yourselves to a drink. I just carry on kissing, I could happily kiss Kriss all day. That feeling is priceless.

They make their way back to the front room.

'So what's this all about Jen?' It's over to Shelly.

'Girls, just to let you all know we're having a baby.'

Leona's jumping round well happy. Claire's like 'who's the dad?'

'He's not about' Shelly says. Claire carries on, saying 'don't worry we're here for you.'

'That's big things. Wot did your mum say Shelly?' I ask.

'You know summit Jen, I thought she would go mad, but she was all right and little Mark's well happy he's gonna be a uncle.'

'I'm so glad everything's kool.'

We're having a laugh about names cos some people give their kids off-key ones like, Bluebell, Hitler - I mean who the fuck in their right mind would name their baby after such a wanker?

It's getting late now, so everyone's gonna stay the night . We got the room, why not? Claire and Leona are gonna stay in the front room and Shelly and Sonia are gonna sleep in the twins' room. I go an get some bedding, say night and take Kriss with me and shut my door. I'm so wrecked I start to undress Kriss. It's a bit of a thrill knowing they're all next door, but I don't care. I want him so badly. Wot has he done to me? Wotever it is I love it.

When I wake up in the morning my clothes are all over the place,

'Wot happened last night?'

'Don't you remember, you were a bad girl!' He starts chuckling to himself.

'Wot did I do?' when he told me, I just had to laugh,

'I'm sorry I don't know where that came from, I was a bit pissed.'

'A bit pissed! You was an animal, you were on fire last night.' Kriss sits up. He's got scratches down his back. 'Babe look what I done to you!' I say in shock.

'I told you, you was an animal last night babe, you let loose, it was amazing! You do something to me girl and I like, I like a lot!'

He goes out the room an I'm laying here thinking, fucking hell what happened? I can remember little bits. I know we had fun! I've fallen for him big style. He comes back in the room.

'I've gotta go babe gotta drop this cash off, I'll see you later.'

'OK babe.' he kisses me and heads off, I haven't felt this good in a long time. I roll over and go back to sleep.

When I finally get up the house is empty, everyone's gone. There's a note near the kettle saying 'Hi hun thanks for a lovely night, you're so funny? Luv ya xx p.s see you later'. Wot do they mean, I'm so funny?

I make tea and go and sit down, trying to think wot went down last night. I know, me and Kriss...I see a little flashback. Shit, I was naughty, I think I done things last night that I don't normally do. The only other person I've ever slept with was Arron. Yer we had sex everywhere back then, it was all new to me, I didn't really know anything, I was young. We tried whole heap of different things, and yer it was good! It's all I knew, but Kriss, he does stuff that blows my mind. I know he's been with nuff girls, cos of the way he is in between the sheets. He knows wot he's doing and I just go with the flow, and trust me the flow is good, it's real good.

My phone rings, it's Kriss, oh my gosh wot's he gonna say?

'Ello darling.'

'Hiya babe' I say.

'Have you remembered yet?'

'Bits and pieces.'

'I can't get last night out of my head Jen, you were amazing. Where did it all come from?'

'I don't know babe, maybe it has summit to do with being with you.'

'I hope so. I'm gonna see you soon, thinking bout you always' he says.

'Bye baby.' We end the call.

He must think I'm a right waste gal, I can't even remember wot I did last night, but I'm not a big drinker and I put away a fair bit. I know I enjoyed myself so it all good!

I go an have a shower, it's nice an hot. I must have been in there for half an hour at least. I grab a towel and wrap it round myself, I'm looking at my body in the mirror, thinking how the hell did I pull Kriss? People have always told me I'm a pretty girl, and yer I'm all right! I'm thinking about cutting my hair, it's long and dark, well halfway down my back, and I've got freckles all over my face. I've always been told I'm lucky to look the way I do and that I could have anybody.

Can it work?

The last time I wanted someone, well look how that turned out! I thought I was in love with Arron. Well at the time, I did love him in my own little way. He tried to play me and got caught out, there was a baby involved and then there wasn't. And now he's dead.

I don't think Kriss would do me like that. My sister Marie once told me all men cheat, is that for real? Surely not! I hope not. I don't see why people can't just talk about their feelings. I understand sometimes people pick the wrong person, and their head gets turned by someone, and they wanna go there! Why can't they just be up front? Then it's up to that person if they stay or go about their business, but give them the chance.

Now Shelly, 19 years old and up the duff with a man twice her age and a wotless one at that. Them kinda men make me sick, out for wot they can get, easy come easy go, how the fuck is all that shit all right?

I mean talking is the key. If you as a person ain't happy where you're at in life be up front and get out. A bit of me understands why Shelly's not gonna tell him. I can't blame her, wot the fuck can he do for her? He can't even do nuffin for hisself and his wife's a tramp after she dunno wot he's about. And wot about the kids? He's already got it's a joke man, you don't treat people like that, so we'll all pull together her for.

Sonia's just floating through life. She needs to sort out her shit, cos when the baby gets here she can't be hanging on no more. She and her family have been through enough, her mum had a hard time, back in the day!

I remember one day after school, we went round there we all clubbed together and brought a bag of weed, our first ever draw. So we're in Shelly's bedroom trying to stick the rizla and we hear a scream. I've never been so scared and trust me it takes a lot to get me shook. We all rushed down the stairs to find Shelly's dad Trevor had knocked out Kellie, that's Shelly's mum, and was kicking her calling her a fucking bitch, he was on one, I remember shouting at him to get off her. Well I didn't word it like that though, it was more like 'wot the fuck have you done you prick get fucking off her', summit like that. The police came and carted him off and he weren't allowed back to the house after that. We used to go round nearly every day to make sure he didn't turn up. If he did we were gonna fuck him up, we didn't care who he was. Shelly's mum was never the same after that,

All of us helped her raise Mark so he looks up to us girls, he's only just turned 12. He's lovely, a proper little man. He was getting bullied at one stage but we sorted that shit one time, now no one can even look at him in the wrong way, so yer, we're there for him always.

That was kinda when I saw people for wot they were, and that's why I have trouble letting people in, cos all they do is hurt ya in the end. So this thing with Kriss, truth is I fell for him a long time ago but he was way out of my league. Anyway he was seeing one girl, to tell you the truth I can't even remember her name. I hated her cos she had wot I wanted, but he would never look at me, I was a yout. So over the years I built this wall around myself. Sometimes even now I look at him and I'm right back there, this little kid who hangs out with his sister.

When I reached about 17 I noticed he was watching me a bit differently. I would catch him looking at me most of the time and I liked it, but I couldn't do nuffin about it. They just lost their mum to cancer, it was a really sad time in all our lives. Kriss went off the rails, girls all over the place. He just didn't give a fuck about anything, and that's when I met Arron.

I should never have gone there, he was trouble from the start, but you really don't see it when you're in it, You think its love, but really it was stupidity on my part. We were together about a year and you know the rest, it didn't end too good. But so is life. After that me and Claire grew closer, we was with each other most of the time, a right pair of bitches. We would get pissed and go out and look for trouble an we got into a hole heap of shit. We were slipping and Kriss was fixing up. I used to go round there just to get a glimpse of him, and wot I saw I liked, but I knew he would never look at me. The way I was going on I was horrible, not a nice person at all. I used to move with them mans backa Brixton, not a good look. Fighting, robbing, we weren't a gang or nuffin like that, just friends getting up to fuckry tings, things you wouldn't ever want your daughter doing.

Then one day a light came on. I didn't want that kinda life no more, I needed to clean up my act fast otherwise wot was the point? So that's wot I done, looking back. Things really do happen for a reason. Them mans now, well most of them are dead. There's kids out there that won't ever know their dads. That's wot you get living a life on road. Yes it's sad and it hurts, but life does go on, and it's wot you make it, and I intend to make it a good 'un.

If you could mould the perfect man, I mean draw him out of thin air as you would want him to be, you'll end up with Kriss every time. Sometimes I think he can't be real. How can someone be so lovely in every way? If his mum could see him she would be so proud. He had to fight to keep Claire with him, well there's no other family members, they are totally on their own apart from their dad. He's somewhere doing summit. They don't know him anyway, but that's not the point, they needed him and where was he? Nowhere. But trust me, Kriss has done a blinder. They are really nice people and I feel lucky to be in their lives.

Someone's at the door and I go and answer it, some Jehovah's

Witnesses preaching the lord's name. I just look at them and say 'no thanks luv' and shut the door. I don't care about them, they got too much time on their hands man, I can't be dealing with that shit, do you know what I mean, fuck sake!

Seeing Leona last night really bought things home to me. These last few days have been special, but I have to remember I've got things to do, shit to sort out. If that man thinks he's got away with things, trust he's not gonna know wot hit him.

I'm a nice enough girl, you know the kind. We grew up with nuffin. When we was little I always felt like the odd one out. Not saying my parents loved me any differently, cos I see now they didn't. I'm the middle child, two older two younger. I remember when there was a school trip to France I needed some things, cos I didn't have nothing halfway decent. My parents didn't really have any money but mum went out shopping, she came back with these shoes. First look I liked them, blood red and shiny. As mum went to take out the other shoe, she told me the other ones not the same, it's a different red. When she took it out it was bright red! She said it will have to do, and I did wear them, I had no choice; I just tried to hide one foot! Yer right, like no one noticed, but I did. The other kids always had nice things and I wanted that, why couldn't I?

From then I got into so much trouble, dropped out of school basically. did wotever I wanted. That's when I found the streets. When it's during the day things seem all right - well if you don't know what's going on out there you'll miss it like it didn't even happen. Everyday people, haven't got a clue wot's really going on out there. Come night time it's a whole new world, things happen you wouldn't believe. I mean some of the things I've seen would make you physically sick.

I remember this one

The things I've done! Even now my mind is really calculated. I'm not easy, I can't just let this slide (the Marcus ting). Just cos you see a girl all little and pretty don't think say she can't do you summit. Them mans in Brixton showed me how to handle myself, which I am grateful for. There is a dark side to me, well I think everyone's got one.

At the time when shit's going down I used to be the first one on it, no matter what it was, the badder the person the better, wot! Imagine some hard ass bad man? So he feels (jokers trying to play bad man). Doing his thing try to fuck over the wrong people. When crunch time come he see me walk in all sweet and pretty, he thought all his Christmases had come at once init? He was in the back room, that's the money room, next man could never get in there but me, easy! Nothing to it, it was a piece of piss, like taking money off a granny.

I won't ever forget that night. Some fuckup shit happened. I ended up blindfolding that fucker, making him believe I was sent as a birthday surprise (it's all in the planning, man!) His boys just let me in. Just show them a little flesh, job done.

Anyway I got the guy (his name was Troy) to send his boys out for an hour or so, then we could get down and dirty. Trust me when I say he was so up for it, he was joke! I took some coke laced with sleeping pills to get him a bit out of it so I could get on with things. I go over to the desk and lean over just a little, just enough, butt out and everything, and got him to take the coke out of my bra with his teeth (I had to play the part). A bit of the bag was hanging out so he didn't really touch me, I'm telling ya he was gagging for it!

I formed two fat lines of Charlie for him - well after all it was his birthday. I put a touch of coke on the back of my hand, he couldn't see how much, he was too busy looking at my body. I must say though I did look fucking hot, well if you want a job done you do it right.

So I took wot was on my hand, it was practically nuffin, and he done the two lines, backing it with some champagne. He was getting kinda fruity trying ah ting. I told him to come sit, I'm gonna give him a lap dance, then wotever he wanted. He was so up for it, nasty fuck, he came and sat and ran his hand down my side. It made me feel sick to have him touch me, dirty dog.

I said I'm gonna blindfold you, he's like na I need to see this. I say don't worry your feel me babe and in a bit you can take it off, and see wot a lucky boy you are.

I take my stockings off slowly one by one. The first one I use to tie one hand down. He was looking a bit lean up, egging me on. The other one I teased him a bit, really made him believe I was on that tip, and then I tied off his hand, making sure he couldn't get out, slip the blindfold down. Now he was ready, and so was I.

I went and opened the front door and let Claire in, we have a quick chat. I told her don't say nuffin, just follow my lead. She was like kool. Now we're back in the room. We ain't got long before his boys are back. He was getting a bit impatient asking wot's going on.

With that I hit him with his own bat, I think I broke his nose. He took it too well, so I hit him again, blood all down his shirt, teeth on the floor. He was like, please, spitting blood everywhere. Claire's looking for the cash, there's some out but we know there's more. And the drugs.

I hit him again across his knees, he starts screaming like a bitch. Shut your fucking mouth I won't say it again, now where is it? He didn't waste no time. 'In the safe, in the safe man!'

'Wot's the fucking code bruv?'

He must have been hurting, cos he gave it up one time. Wot, is it there fam? She nodded, kool let's go. We just left him sitting there like some prick, fuck know wot his people thought when they walked in.

That's wot I'm saying, don't fuck with people you don't know, cos you never know when it's gonna come back and bite. Troy was lucky, he gave it up easy. Nuffin was ever mentioned about that. Do you really think he could ever tell anyone the truth about wot really happened that night? That one girl come run up on him and robbed him? He would be taken for a dickhead.

I had already taken him out of business, he didn't need the shame of that as well. We're from different ends, and anyway I don't even look like that - bare make up, weave, high heels and shit, that ain't me, so yer, I can handle myself every time.

That's the life I wanted so much to leave behind. I thought them days were long gone, but I find myself here again fighting someone else's battles. This is it, the last thing I do! I have to start living my own life for myself.

I go into the front and sit down, not proud of wot I've done in the past, thinking back I done some messed up things. I don't like me much when I'm like that, but Leona... I just can't drop it.

I reach for my phone and find Marcus in my phone book. Should I? 'Fuck it' I think. So I ring it, it rings a few and then a guy answers.

'Hello?'

'Hiya, is that David?'

'Na, who's this?'

'It's Lacey man, stop mucking about.'

'Na' he says.

'So when he gonna be back?'

'Na babes, this ain't David's phone. I don't know no David.'

'So who's this I'm talking to? You sound kinda nice, wot's your name?'

'Marcus' he says. 'Sorry wot's your name babe?'

'Lacey.' I say sorry for troubling him, say bye and hang up.

Do you know how hard that was for me, talking all nice like I find him attractive? But it's all good, cos now that leaves it open for me to call again.

I get a text off Kriss, *I'll be with you soon babe, do you want anything? x* Sent one back, *No thanks babe x just yourself x*

Once I sort out that thing, I can get back to normal and be the person Kriss needs, the girl I want to be. When I'm with him I can be myself, no need for any acts. He's seen me at my worst, and it wasn't a pretty sight I can tell ya, but when he's around the person I am is really nice. I like it, I think I'm growing up!

I fling something on, fix up my hair. Well, I say fling something on, it took me time finding something. I make a cuppa and put the telly on, there's a spliff in the ashtray. I light it and doze off.

Bitter sweet

A while later the door goes and it's Kriss. I let him in, feeling all sleepy. He wraps his arms around me and kisses me. Oh my god, you know that feeling when the whole of your body knows it's alive, that warm tingle from the top of your head to the tips of your toes feeling? He pulls away, I'm like drifting, head back, wishing he hadn't stopped.

'Come Jen, let's go to mine babe.'

'OK' I say. I love spending time round there, the way he's done it up it's proper nice. You don't really see yards like that, well not where I come from. It's not over the top or nuffin like that, it's just nice. You walk in and the front room off to the left is all white with black gloss trim, wooden flooring.

Anyway we arrive at his, we go in. There's a light on down the hall. Come, he said. Wot's going on, I'm thinking to myself that's the spare room? I follow him in and it was so beautiful, if you ever see it man, it brought a tear to my eyes.

I look at Kriss and like a fool I couldn't help myself. I got a bit upset, well maybe upset is the wrong word, emotional, that's the word I'm looking for. He makes me feel so special. He had set up a table, it was gorgeous,

'How did you manage to do all this?' I said. 'I love it.'

'I just wanted to do something for you, this is it babe' he said as he pulls my chair out.

'I know it's early days, but the way you are and the way you make me feel Jen, honestly since mum died there's been a big hole. It's been really hard trying to keep things afloat, not only for me, I had Claire to consider as well. Sometimes I would think wot's the point. Every day was a struggle. All right I've got nice things around me, and yer there's been girls in and out, which I'm not proud off, but this, you, I knew it was you for time but you're so hard faced sometimes, you can't see wot's starring you in the face. I've been trying for a while but you kept knocking me back.'

He looks at me and says, 'Jen it hurt, you know I could never impress you.'

'Kriss it ain't even that.'

'Wot then?' he asks. I carry on talking.

'I fancied you from the first I see you, but I was a kid. When your mum passed away, that's when I should have been there for you, but I didn't even do that.'

'Na don't say that babe, I was out there doing a whole heap of stuff! Things I don't even want you to know about, but if you want I'll tell you.'

I give him one of them looks, like, *right!*

'I will Jen, I ain't gonna hide nuffin, I don't wanna mess this up babe.'

'You won't, I'm here cos I wanna be.'

We eat, the food is so good. One day I'll be plating food as nice as that. The wine's hitting all the right spots. He pours me another glass and hands me a joint, now I'm rocking, mash up. Half my hair's fallen down. Kriss comes over and takes the clip out and runs his fingers through it, I'm buzzing hard. I'm on the chair, Kriss swings me round and goes on his knees, making us the same height. He parts my legs an moves in for that snug fit. We're kissing, I feel light headed, he leads the way to his room and locks the door. He steps towards me and lifts my chin a little. He plants a kiss on me, touching me, making me feel like I've never wanted someone so bad. The kissing is deep and meaningful. We move slowly to the bed (king size four poster) tugging at each other's clothes, not being able to keep our hands off each other. I am a bit pissed but the way I'm feeling fucking hell, is this it (love)? It has to be, I hope it is!

We're on the bed enjoying each other touching, kissing. The way he kisses my body it's magic, pure magic, if you've never felt this feeling you've got it all to come. I just hope you enjoy it as much as I do.

In the background I can hear my phone ringing, but trust, whoever it is I don't wanna know. He starts to touch me very intimately. His touch is so soft, my body moves in waves. 'Ahh babe' he says, kissing me up.

He watches me watching him. I run my hands over his body, I can feel all his muscles rippling. I'm so turned on right now, I don't want the night to end, it's like one of them movies where everything's perfect, the main characters are hot. You know the type, good looking, nice yard, nice things, everything just as it should be, not like real life!

I mean people wish for things like that to happen. We all know movies are made that way to get us all hooked, but it doesn't stop us hoping that's there's a life out there for all of us. We just have to find our own path.

He draws hisself to his knees and shuffles me down to him; he leans through my open thighs, kissing me, asking 'You OK babe?' I kiss him to reassure him I'm fine.

He lifts me from the base of my back and enters me slowly, I take a deep breath. We take it nice an slow. I'm enjoying every minute. He's running his hands all over me, looking at me, telling me how good I feel, how beautiful I am. Maybe it's partly to do with having wanted each other for so long, and now we've finally got together the sweeter it is. The unknown makes us experiment. We're finding out about each other, wot makes us tick, and trust he makes me tick and all the rest is a bonus!

He's moving his body back and forth nice and slowly. I'm trying to contain myself. 'Yer baby, do you like that?' he says. I can't even speak, he's got me twisted. He lifts my legs just a bit, just enough so he can reach to kiss me. The pleasure he gives me is outta this world.

He pulls out for a minute, we're still kissing. He starts to kiss my neck, down to my breast, he's handling me so softly! His touch makes me want him even more. How can that be possible? We're enjoying each other so much if someone told me I was gonna die tomorrow I wouldn't care cos I would die happy.

He kisses me on the lips. 'Ready for round two?' he says.

'Oh yer.'

He takes my hand and puts it down where I find a bit of him that's really happy to feel me. I line us up and with a little movement he's in. Now things have changed. Round one was a warm up, round two we're getting down, believe that. It's like he's gone deeper, the way his body's moving, thrusting into me. It's turned a bit hardcore. It hurts a little, but it's a nice pain. The thrill is overwhelming. He turns me over so now I'm on my hands and knees and he's doing his thing. I didn't really like it, it's uncomfortable for me, I've been out of action for a long time, but I can see Kriss likes it, so I try and take it, well for as long as I can.

I pull away and he lies down. I climb on top, kissing him, and guide him in. His hands are round my bum, drawing me down. I like to be in control. I make it so just the top half of him is in, short sharp moves, I can see the colour rushing to his lips, his eyes holding so much pleasure as he looks at me.

'I'm gonna come babe, I can't hold back no more' he says. Moving up and down slowly, I move all the way down and round. That's it, all over.

I lie on him awhile, I can't fucking move. I feel his arms go around me as he kisses my shoulder. I'm shagged out, we were at it for hours.

I feel lucky

I must have fallen asleep. That was the best night ever! I'm a bit sore but I had a brilliant night and I'll remember it, every bit.

I wake up to an empty bed. I can hear someone next door so I get up and go and have a look, bless him he's tidied up from last night.

'Morning babe' he says, arms out. I go an snuggle into him. Wot man does all the clearing up? He ain't just a pretty face, in his mind he's a lot older than his years!

'Tea, beautiful?' he says, smiling. 'Yes please.' We go into the kitchen, it's wicked in there. His kettle's well nice, you fill it up turn it on and just put your cup under the spout and it pours itself. My dad would love it.

He's asking me about the Leona thing, I keep him updated with what's going on.

'Babe listen, I know she's your girl and you want to sort it yourself, just let me put two man on that, it can be dealt with' he says.

'Na Kriss, I need to do this.'

'Well I'll send the mans with you' he says, putting his arms round me.

'Babe, if I weren't with you I would still have to sort it.'

'Na, I still know ya, so don't even go there babe. We'll see how it pans out. If you need the help you come to me, cos if anything happened to you, boy that would be a madness in itself babe.'

'Stop it!' I say. 'Nuffin gonna happen and yer, if I need you I'll let you know.' I plant a smacker on him.

I go and jump in the shower and Kriss joins me. He starts washing me, sliding his soapy hands all over my body. It's really nice, I've never shared a shower before. We kiss under the water, wicked feeling. We have a play around, laughing and giggling.

'Wot you on today babe?' he asks.

'Not sure yet.' I get dressed, Kriss makes me summit to eat. I am lucky, he does look after me! I check my phone - a message from Mum, *hi Jennie its mum, been trying to get hold of you, hope your OK were coming home the day after tomorrow can you call me when you get this x mum x*

I give her a call, they're all right. She just wants to come home. She told me off for not phoning her enough, if only if she knew wot I had been up to.

I tell Kriss they're due back tomorrow. He's like 'nice' It don't really affect us after all, he's got his own place, we don't have to run round and hide.

But they will like him. My mum's always said, that boy Kriss he's lovely Jen, you could do far worse. Every time he dropped off or picked up Claire, Mum would be there stirring. she's so funny. So I'm hoping Mum will be kool and if she's kool Dad will be all right.

Well let me tell you a bit about my dad. He's a cockney black guy, came over here when he was like seven from Jamaica, bought up over the East End of London. Back then times were hard, he was the only black kid in his school. Imagine how hard that would have been, being called monkey boy, spade, things like that? A seven year old boy. He had it hard, they moved to Brixton. Not sure of the year but he was still a yout. In his teens every day he was pulled over by the police, stop and search, shit! Being called fucking wogs and sunshine just for the fun of it, but my dad's kool man, oh but he can chat for England believe, so when he meets Kriss I'm gonna leave them to it.

'I gotta go home and tidy round the place' I say. Kriss is like 'I'll drop you off babe.'

'I need to go check Jay, them mans are back today.'

'Kool nice one darling.'

We jump in the car. 'I hate it when I have to leave you Jen.'

'Me too babe, but you got things to do. I don't want to get in the way of that.'

'We'll make it work.' He pulls up at mine.

'Stay safe for me.' I kiss him.

'I'll bell you, sweetheart' and he drives off.

I go in, put the heating on, warm up this place, get the Hoover out and give the place a quick going over. Do a bit of dusting and put a wash on, then I lie down on the sofa.

The door goes, I go an answer it, it's Kriss with the most beautiful bunch of roses. He puts them in my hand and kisses me all lovingly, jumps in his car and off he goes. About 20 mins later I get a text. All it says is *as beautiful as u xxx*

How fucking sweet, never did I think anything like this could happen to me. Claire phones, she's popping over for a bit, I have a little sleep. I'm tired, I just crash on the sofa.

I can hear the door. I don't wanna move, I have to drag myself up to answer it, I'm hanging like I went out last night!

It's Claire. 'Wot gawn, Jen?'

'Hiya babe where you been?' I say.

'Out and about, you'll never guess who I see last nite.'

'Who?' I say rubbing my eyes!

'Maggie. If you ever see her, Jen.'

'Wot, did she see you?'

'Yer but she might as well not have. She was begging a change, rotten dirty filthy blood. I tried to talk to her. In the end she pissed me off and I just left her.'

'Wot you sayin, just left her. Na fam, you don't do that.'

'Jen, you don't get wot I'm sayin.'

'Shit man, I'm gonna have to let Delroy know.'

'How was your night anyway?' she asks.

'I had a wicked time, Kriss is lovely.'

'He's all right, he loves you init?' she says.

'I hope so! Let's make tea, we need to talk.'

'Why wot's up?'

'I phoned Marcus yesterday.'

'And?'

'Well we had a chat, sort of.'

'Wot happened, come on Jen, spill!'

'Not a lot was said really, I asked for some random guy and took it from there, so I kinda left it open for me to ring again.'

'Shit Jen, so things are moving! Why didn't you wait for me to be here for support?'

'I know, but Leona was on my mind, summit just told me to phone! I told Kriss I just want to be up front with him, do ya know what I mean?'

'Yer that's good, what did he say?'

'You know him Claire.'

'I bet he said he'll sort it out for you, init?'

'Yer, summit along them lines. He made me swear if I need him I mustn't feel no way he'll get some of the mans on board.'

'So wot, plans changed?'

'Na, tings are still running.'

We have our tea. 'Sorry babe, I really need to sleep' I tell her.

'I'm going to check Naz, he's got something for me. Laters, babe.'

'See you soon, I wonder wot that's about?'

I curl up on the sofa and drift. The house ain't gonna be quiet for much longer. In a way though I'm glad. When everyone's home they drive me mad, I can't stand it. I mean, they really fucking piss me off. The twins are at that age they're in everything, digging up in my room when I'm out, taking my things, breaking stuff, they make me sick most of the time, but I've missed them all so much.

Things are gonna be different when they get back.

I wake up to screaming, a high-pitched screaming. My heart's racing. I go to the window and have a look.

There's a young black girl across the road, crouched over something, screaming her head off. I don't know why, I just grab my coat and run out there. The whole street is empty, when I say no one came out I mean no one. Community, wot fucking community, curtains twitching, that's all you get. I phone 999 but I can see the boy's dead.

I take off my coat and put it over his little face. He must only be about 15, I think to myself. I try to get the girl away but she ain't having it and who could blame her, so I just leave her and wait.

It took them about 15 mins before anyone got there. The girl's covered in blood, all snot running down her face. The police put her in the car and take her away from the scene.

They're asking me a whole heap of things. I just tell them I didn't see anything, I live on the road and heard her screaming, that's it, that's all I know, and I phoned the emergency services.

They start putting their tape up. The officer asks whose jacket was on the victim, I say it's mine. He's like 'We're gonna hang on to it for now, forensic will want to take a look, but we will get it back to you at some stage.'

'Na that's all right, bin it.' (I can't wear that again, tho I loved that jacket, it cost me money, still.)

They take my details and I go in, fucking hell wot the fuck! I text my mum and tell her wot just happened, and maybe it's best to stay one more day. She phones me.

'Jen, are you all right?'

'Yer mum, don't come tomorrow there's police everywhere, it's not nice.'

'OK babe, but we'll be home the day after. But are you all right?'

'Yer. I'm gonna go stay at our mate's tonight.'

'Yes, I think that's the best thing to do, love you darling.'

'Bye mum' I say and hang up.

I phone Kriss and let him know what happened and that old bill are

116

everywhere, he tells me he's on his way, he don't ever carry anything on him, never. He was with me in like five mins. 'Come babes you can't stay here, we'll go to mine.' I grab a few things and we leave.

'You all right though babe?'

'Yer I'm kool.' We stop off at the chippie. When we get to his we go inside and he makes me tea.

'I'm all right, go and do wot you're doing' I tell him.

'Na, Jay can sort it.' I give him a hug. 'Go' I say.

'You sure babe?'

'Yer, I just wanna go bed.'

Is she a fool?

He follows me through and puts the telly on, kisses me and says he won't be long. I eat my chips, I hear the door, and go check. It's Claire, looking a bit shady.

'Jen you scared the life out of me' she says, kinda looking around to see who's in.

'Why wot you doing, wot's in the bag?'

'Shh where's Kriss?' I'm looking at her, not sure wot to think.

'Not here, wot is it Claire?' She's like 'come'. We go to her room, she puts the bag down.

'Wot you got in there? Stop fucking around.'

I open it. Handcuffs! 'Wot the fuck are you doing Claire?' I see a sawn-off lying there. 'Why you got that you fool? You best get it out of here before your brother gets back, you know he don't roll like that. Shit man!'

'Jen, he ain't no saint.' I don't know who she thinks she's talking to!

'Don't even bother, hold on a fucking minute, shut up! Fucking hell you don't bring them things in the yard. Who you think you are, get it out now, whose is it?'

'Naz's' she says, like it's nuffin.

'You ain't got no right bringing that ere. Wot if the police kick off the door?'

'I didn't even think about that one. Jen wot am I going do?'

'You need to take it back. Kriss is coming back soon, you best move that.'

'I'll take it now.' I keep telling this girl think first (understand).

'Do you want me to bop with you?'

'Yer, come then.' We leave, here I go again. I tell her wot happen outside mine, she couldn't believe it.

'Are you all right though babe?'

'Yer man, I don't know wot's happening any more. Then you turned up with that thing, wot was you thinking? You best wipe that down before you give it back.'

'Na, I haven't handled it.'

'I hope not, you know you can get like five years for handling that g! And you don't even know who had that or wot they done with it.'

'I just thought I would get it and put it down in case.'

'In case of wot fam?'

'That thing, Jen.'

'Na man, I'm not on it like that. So wotever you was thinking, think again. I told you you're not in this! Wot's wrong with you?'

We reach Naz's house. I ain't too happy with him, I bang the door. He's like 'Jen babe.' I put the bag in his hand and he looks all puzzled and that. I say 'Don't ever understand' and walk off. 'Na Jen, sorry man.'

We're walking back. 'Wot's wrong with you, I just see a yout dead on the floor and there's you walking road with them things, fuck sake Claire you need to check yourself and fix up!'

We reach the house. Kriss's car's there!

'Now look, I'm gonna have to lie, it's a good thing I found it when I did.'

'I'm sorry Jen, I know you're right. Are you gonna say anything to Kriss?'

'You gonna do it again?'

'Na, swear down.'

'Then he don't need to know, not from me anyway. Plus it's sorted, don't let me down.'

We go in, Kriss is there looking a bit uneasy. 'Where you two been?'

'We went for a walk round the block.'

'Wot, you couldn't take your phone babe?

'Na. Sorry, I just needed to clear my head I thought I had it.'

He cuddles me. We go through to the kitchen where he makes me tea and rolls me a joint and hands it to me. Claire's in her room, don't think she can face Kriss right now.

'Shall we watch a film?' he asks.

'Like wot?'

'Wotever you want, babe. Comedy?'

'Na, I'm not in a laughing mood, sorry babe. I'm not good company am I?'

'Well you've been through the mill tonight, so I understand.' He's so caring. We go and sit in the front room and he puts some music on (slow jams) then comes and puts his arms around me.

'Babe, I don't like seeing you like this.'

'I'm all right. It's just when you see stuff like that it makes you think about things, you know, question stuff.'

'Wot do you mean Jen?' He looks at me a bit funny.

'Na babe not like that, not you! I'm glad you're in my life, wouldn't have it any other way.'

'But he was just a yout, his poor mum, wot must she been going through.' I get a bit upset.

'Don't babes, come ere.' He holds me. 'You don't know wot happened tonight, babe. You just see the aftermath, you don't know wot he dun, wot he was up to. For all you know he could have been a little shit. You know that saying, what happens in the dark always comes out in the light? Things happen Jen, and we just have to deal with it the best we can.'

Wot are we all doin?

I know it's true, but it's still hard to get your head round do you know wot I mean? I know nuff mans out there who are waste mans, but this one was a baby, he hadn't even started living his life yet. It's just a shame that's how things are on road. The way things are it makes me feel I don't want kids, not living here anyway. I mean them mothers out there give birth to their little bundles of joy and put so much love into them, watching them grow into decent human beings, and then some tosser comes along and takes all that away from them just like that. People take shit too far now days, guns and knives, why? If you don't like someone, stay the fuck away, simple, get me? Life's too short man, people need to open their eyes. This isn't a movie, it's life! Some people deserve a good kickin. But to end a life, that's just one step too far.

We go to his bedroom, I'm feeling a little down. Things are starting to get to me. I take my clothes off and jump in bed. Kriss rolls up and we smoke and have a kiss and cuddle, he always make things seem just that bit easier.

I must have drifted off, I remember Kriss saying something, wot about I don't even know. I wake up with him still holding me. I just lie there thinking that I am one of the lucky ones. Some people go their whole life not ever finding the right one. I know people who are in relationships but they're not happy, they just make do with wot they got or cheat. Why though? We all have one life, why waste it? If you're not happy with the cards you've been dealt, change your hand, move on and start again.

It's just the way it goes sometimes. I understand why Kriss don't want me to go ahead with this Marcus thing, but I always had to stick up for myself, I can't be having someone fighting my battles, it just comes naturally. So is life! You do wot needs to be done to a certain level still.

I get up an Claire's in the kitchen. 'Morning Jen! Naz has been on the phone, he says he needs us to go round ASAP.'

'Why, wot's going on?'

'Dunno, he just said can we go round.'

I can't be bothered with that. He's just gonna chat shit in my ear and I don't want to hear it right now. With that I hear Kriss calling me. I go through.

'Morning darling' I say as I jump on the bed for cuddles.

'Hi babe' he says, all sleepy faced. 'I wanna take you somewhere today.'

'OK, where we going?'

'You'll see, get ready, yer?'

I'm a bit puzzled, don't know wot's going on. We get ready and leave, he's not really saying much. We've been driving for a while. There's a signpost (Watford).

'Wot we doing here Kriss?'

'There's someone I want you to meet.'

'OK, who is it?'

'A good friend' he says and leaves it at that.

I look at him. 'Are you in trouble?'

'Na babe, I just need you to meet him. Why you worried?'

'No it's just...' I start to say but he jumps in 'You'll understand when we get there babe, its nuffin to be scared of.'

'I'm not scared, I just don't get it.'

'You will.'

We drive down a slip road for about 20 minutes, then Kriss parks up outside this big fuck-off yard. 'Here we are babe, come.'

I'm getting out of the car, really unsure what's happening. I know Kriss would never hurt me, so wot's all this about?

Kriss makes a call. He's like, 'yer it's me!' A few minutes later the door opens, there's some guy standing there waiting for us.

'Come! You must be Jen. I'm Mackie' he says, kissing me on both cheeks. He turns to Kriss. 'Nice man, real nice. You kool though bruv?'

'Yer, sweet as mate' Kriss replies with that manly hug ting they do (men that is). We go through, I give Kriss the evil eye, like to say wot's going on? If you ever see this yard, oh my gosh the man is flexing, I can't believe it. He's white, in his fifties, a real cockney,

'So Jen, sit lets ave a chat.' Kriss just leaves the room.

'Chat about wot?' I don't like the fact he know certain things man.

'Your friend an wot happened to her, don't ave a pop at Kriss, he loves ya. He's given me some details on the guy you're looking for, I've ad a shufty round. Don't worry, I work on my own. Jus to let ya know all right? You don't need to know wot I'm about, I've known your geezer for years, he's a fucking diamond. The reason you're ere is cos I found him! So wot do you want done?'

'I don't need your help, thanks' I say (stubborn little shit that I am).

'Jen mate, Kriss is tryin his best for ya yer? So it don't matter wot you say, I know you don't wanna hear it but it's out of your hands now, so ya need to let me know how ya wanna play this, yer?'

'Where's Kriss?'

'He'll be back in a minute. He's doin this for you, yer? Not sayin ya can't sort it out for yourself, no one's saying that, but he don't want that kinda life for ya, understand?'

'I see where you're coming from. I'm starting to see it from Kriss's point of view.'

'But that's my girl.'

'I said I would sort it, not being funny or nuffin but I don't even know you bruv! And now you're telling me, na, it ain't working like that. I need to talk to Kriss.'

I walk towards the door and reach for the handle, talk to Kriss, and then we'll have our chat. I leave the room and take a minute. Wot the fuck, I can hear some music. I follow the sound, pop my head round the door. There's Kriss.

'Babe wot you doing? Why didn't you just say how you were feeling?'

'Come babe.' We go and sit he turns to me.

'Jen, you're too headstrong sometimes. I thought it would be best not to say anything, just sort it out, bring you up here to meet Mackie and take it from there. I know your pissed off right now I did it this way cos I care, I love you, you're not on your own no more darling. If I can do summit to make your life easier I will.'

'Kriss I understand why you did wot you done, but...'

'Na Jen, there's no buts. This way there's no comeback, ya get me? So you need to get back in there and tell him wot's to be done, yer?'

I go back to Mackie. 'You spoke to Kriss and sorted it?' he says.

'Yer' I said. 'so wot then, we doing this?'

'Mackie, I just want him to pay for wot he done, nuffin over the top, just hurt.'

'All right. I'll get a message to ya when it done.'

'As soon as.'

With that Kriss walks in. 'All right mate, you gonna stay awhile?' says Mackie.

'Na we got plans. You ready babe, do you wanna wait in the car?'

I say bye to Mackie and he holds on to my hand. 'It's been a pleasure' he says, kissing me on both cheeks like that mafia shit.

I feel a bit funny walking through the house on my own, it feels like I just done a deal with the devil. I get in the car and wait. The door opens, I can see they're close. They say bye, Kriss jumps in the car.

OMG

'You pissed off with me babe?' he asks.

'You know something, I was, but I've had time to think about everything, and the answer to that is no I'm not, you've showed me summit today.'

'Wot, a good thing or bad?'

'Good all the way.'

He smiles and drives off. 'Have you made plans for tonight babe?'

'Na, why?'

'I've booked a hotel, you up for it?'

'Yer of course. But we ain't got no clothes with us, are we gonna go home first?'

'Na, we're gonna go shopping' he says, rubbing my knee.

We stop off and get a bite to eat, then hit the shops. I'm not one of them girls who like to spend other people's money, boyfriend or not. Kriss picks out a really nice dress and high heels. I'm not really into things like that, but if that's how he wants me that's wot he'll have.

At the hotel we're getting ready for wot I don't know. I come out of the bath to see Kriss in a suit, wow I swear down didn't think say he could look any better. He takes my breath away. I walk over and kiss him and fix his tie.

'You look so good.'

'Thanks babe' he says. I grab my dress and shoes and head back to the bathroom. I'm so nervous, it feels like we're big people, doing the things they do. Fuck me, wot's happening? I get dressed and look at myself in the mirror. I can't believe it - I'm beautiful, like one of them women you see and your're hating on her, but this time it's me.

I walk out, Kriss stands up. 'Babe you're gorgeous, look at you.' And I am. I feel like a princess. Never in a million years did I ever think I could look this good.

He kisses me. I've got butterflies. he takes me by the hand all proud and says, 'you ready babe?'

'As ready as I'll ever be.'

We're in the lift waiting for the doors to open. Ping, they open and we leave, and as we're walking through, everyone's looking at us. I feel like a movie star. The doorman tilts his hat and opens the door for us. Kriss tips him and the car park attendant drives up in Kriss's car. He tips him and we get in and drive off, not sure where we're going, but I don't even care as long as we're together. It's only round the corner and we're getting out again (the love nest). I've heard about this place. All the stars come here. The food's meant to be outta this world.

We go in and get shown to our table. The manager comes over and shakes hands with Kriss! He introduces himself to me and leaves us.

'Do you know him?' I ask.

'Yer, I went to school with him. We got a bit of business going on, but we're here to eat not chat shop.'

We order, and while we're waiting the manager sends over a bottle of champagne on the house. Kriss gives him the nod.

'Jen you make me happy you know. I've never done anything like this before so I'm just gonna say it.'

My heart feels like it's gonna explode. 'Wot's wrong babe?' I say.

'Everything's fallen into place since we've started seeing each other, I just want to let you know how much you mean to me babe.' He goes into his pocket and pulls out... a box. 'This is for you babe.'

My hand's shaking. It's a long box.

'Go on, open it.' I pull the lid back. It's a beautiful diamond tennis bracelet, I've always wanted one. I'm feeling a bit choked. He puts it on me, kissing my hand.

'Thank babe, I love it so much.'

Our food arrives. It looks so good I don't want to mess it up. We start eating and Kriss says 'I wanna spend the rest of my life with you Jen. Marry me.'

'Wot?' I'm choking on my salad.

'Drink some water, babe.'

Did he really just say that? I look at him, all tearful eyed.

'What do you say? Be my wife.'

I'm trying to say yes, but the word's not coming out. I take a minute to compose myself.

'I know we ain't been together long but I know you. I want to wake up with you every day, I wanna grow old with you, love you, one day start a family. Wot do you say?'

A hundred things are running through my mind, all good. A tear runs down my face. I'm so happy. Is this really happening to me?

'Well?' he says.

'Of course I will. I love you, let's do this.'

He takes another box out and puts it in front of me and opens the lid. My eyes open wide, I've never seen nuffin like it. Some big rock. For me. My hands fly to my mouth.

'Its beautiful Kriss. Wot have I done to deserve you?'

'It's the other way round Jen, you're my life, my world. Thank you for being you.'

The restaurant is packed, but it feels like we're the only two there, until we hear everyone clapping. I feel so special. How one person can make another so happy?

Kriss gets up and puts the ring on my finger. It fits.

'How did you know my size?'

'Claire helped me out with that one' he says with a wink.

I'm so happy words can't describe how I'm feeling. I know we're only young but I so want this. We kiss and it's wonderful (I always knew it was him as long as I can remember).

He goes on to tell me he's bought into the love nest, so when I've finished college that's where I'll be. Can the night get any better? I'm just a normal girl from the street.

Karl (the manager) comes over to congratulate us and says he's looking forward to us working together. I can't believe wot's going on. I have to pinch myself to make sure this is really happening.

Kriss laughs and asks for the bill, Karl's like 'it's on the house'. They shake hands and we leave and get in the car. Kriss phones Claire, she's well happy.

'We'll see you in the morning sis' he says and he hangs up. We make our way back to the hotel and go to the bar for a drink. I think I'm in shock or summit. Every time I look at my hand I want to run round screaming. We head to our room waiting for the lift, the doors open, we walk in and press the button.

He starts kissing, me running his fingers through my hair, touching my body, me touching him. It feels amazing. We're promised to each other, wicked feeling!

He pulls my hand up and kisses the ring on my finger, looking into my eyes, all the while sayin 'I love you'.

'I love you too baby!'

The door's open and we finally get to our room and open the door. There's flowers everywhere, he amazes me, I don't know how he does it!

I go and lie on the bed. Kriss locks the door and takes his suit jacket off and hangs it up. I'm looking at him, I want him more each time I see him, and he's all mine, we're getting married! Don't know wot my parents will say, but they love me so they will understand.

He comes and joins me on the bed, holding my hand, playing with my ring,

'You happy babe?'

'I really am' I say kissing him. 'When I was a kid I used to dream about you. Well not you but about this day, if I would ever find the one who was made for me. When I met you I felt something, and then, so much happened in both our lives and I let wot I felt for you go.' There's that saying - if you love something let it go.

'And you came back into my life. For a long time I felt like I lost you, so I tried to keep you at arm's length. I was fighting myself! Not really knowing wot I wanted even though I knew it was you Kriss, it's always been you.'

'Babe, I had to make sure you felt the same way. I wish you could have met my mum Jen, she would have loved you so much. They say men go for someone who reminds them of their mother and in a way you're like her, strong minded, a fighter, caring. You give my life meaning. You make me wanna be a better person.'

'Oh babe, that's so sweet' I say,

He helps me take off my dress, I put the radio on, he pulls me for a dance. I feel silly but I go with the flow. I like the way it feels when he holds me, touching me, getting to know my body. We're kissing, we move to the bed, both a bit tiddly catching some joke about the time when he was seeing one girl Emma, she was all right. 'I got on well with her.'

'Jen you didn't like her, stop lying.'

'Na, she was kool' I say.

'Babe stop it, whenever she was at mine you wouldn't leave, I remember you was so funny.'

'Why wot?'

'I knew you had a crush on me, I've got eyes.'

'Wot you saying? Claire talks to me you know.'

''Na babe, she don't chat nuffin like that, she would always drop your name when other girls was at the house.'

'Is it?' I say. 'Emma thought we was up to things.'

'Shut up, swear down?'

'Yer, the day we split up she said if I let you go I would regret it for the rest of my life, she could see there was summit between us. She was right, now I see it. Well, I always knew.' He pulls me close and holds me tight and we lie there listening to the music and sleep.

We wake up and the radio's still on. He looks at me and laughs.

'Wot's funny?' I say, pushing out my lips like a big kid.

'I'm just happy babe, life's good, really good' he says, squeezing me. 'Right, gotta get you home, wot time they due back?'

'This afternoon some time.'

'You gonna tell them?'

'Yer, I'm not hiding you.' He looks at me. 'We'' do it together'

Kriss gets a call, I can hear a guy's voice. He hangs up. 'Jen?

'Yes babe?'

'It's done.'

'Wot's done babe?'

'The thing.'

I sit up and it registers. Marcus. Shit, that's how things are done, just like that, no fucking around? That's his business, wankers like that deserve wot they get I think to myself. I turn to Kriss. He gives me that look like to say it's all over.

I know he wants better for me but what you can't do, someone else can. There's a way around everything. I'm starting to understand that now.

We get ready to leave. I've had the best time. I'll never forget it as long as I live.

I get a text, *We're leaving about lunch time see you soon darling x mum*

'Wot do you wanna do babe, go to mine first? Well should I say ours.' that sounds so nice, ours.

'Yer, let's go.' We leave, and on the way we grab summit to eat. After a bit we pull up at home. Claire comes running out in her pjs, flinging her arms round me.

'Let me see it!' I hold up my hand.

'It's beautiful, you happy babe?'

'Yer' I say, hugging her.

'Where did you get it in the end Kriss?' she asks.

'Hatton Garden.' We go inside, I put the kettle on. I tell Claire all about last nite. she knew about the love nest for a while. She tells me Kriss was planning it for long now, he knew what he wanted all the time, and that he never gave up!

How stupid do I feel? I get a bit upset with myself. With that he walks in.

'I've got to go up the road baby, I won't be long.' he kisses me and leaves.

Keeping things under wraps

Claire's like 'shit Jen, have you spoke to Leona today?'

'Na my phone's dead, why wot's happened?'

'She phoned looking for you.'

'Why?'

'She said summit about the police coming to her house early this morning.'

'For?'

'To find out when she last saw Penny.'

'Is it?'

'Yer, apparently he jumped in front of a train some time this morning.'

'Wot, how they know it was him?'

'Summit to do with a wallet.'

'Swear down, I need to go round to check her, see wah agawn.'

'Let me get dress and I'll come with ya.'

'Kool, you got any weed Claire?'

'Yer, in the box babe.'

I roll a joint, fuck knows I need it! I'm hoping deep down he did jump and it was nuffin to do with me or Mackie.

On the way over there so many things are running through my head. We reach and knock the door, Veronica opens it all happy. 'Come in girls.'

We go into the front room, it come in like a party. Everyone's got a drink and in high spirits. I hear Leona.

'Where you been Jen?'

'Sorry babe, my phone's dead. Wot's going on?'

She sat down. 'The police came this morning.'

'OK. And?'

'They were asking me stuff about Marcus.'

'Yer?'

My heart's going. Does she know?

'They told me there's been an accident. A young black male had jumped out in front of a train and he didn't stand a chance. They know it's him cos they found a wallet with his details in it, but they still need to wait for dental records or summit.'

I'm thinking to myself, did he jump or was he pushed?

'And did I know where his family lives.'

'Wot did you say Leona?'

'Said I don't know them, and I'm sure they're not in this country.'

'So wot now?'

'They said they will be in contact soon as they know more.'

I put my arm round her. 'How are you though?'

'I'm just glad Jen, I know it sound bad but he can't hurt me or anyone else ever again. Hold on, wot's that Jen?'

'Wot babe.' she points to my hand.

'Oh yer, it's not really the time, but I got engaged last nite' I say smiling. 'Mum, come here.'

'Wot is it?' she shouts from the kitchen.

'Come, Jen getting married!'

'Wot, who to?'

'It's Kriss init!'

It's like they all know, and I thought I was playing things down.

'Yer, of course' Claire says. V comes in and has a look.

'It's beautiful, he must love you very much. You must bring him here so I can meet him, all right?'

'Yes mum.'

'Leona, I have to make a move, my mum and that are on their way home, I've gotta go pick a few things up.'

We say bye to everyone and leave, and head to the shops to pick up bread, milk, eggs and loo roll.

'Jen, wot's going on?'

'Wot you talking about Claire?'

'Well when I told you about Penny, it's like you weren't shocked or nuffin. It come in like you knew summit had happened. Wot you sayin babe?'

'Claire, you know say I can't stand him. It's just I'm on such a high about me and Kriss and then Penny gets dropped into the conversation, how do you want me to act? And to top it off he's dead, I can't get my head round it, that's like me saying to you did you have summit to do with it, it's you that went and got a gun. Now wot you saying fam?'

'Na star' she says.

My mind goes wandering. Did he jump or was it done like that to make people think he jumped? The police think that's wot happened.

We get to mine an I put the heating on, it's fucking cold out there, well it's about six weeks till Christmas. I put away the shopping, there's nuffin to do as I done it all the other day.

We head back over to Claire's. I need to smoke. I put my phone on charge. I've got a voice mail, it's my dad, 'We'll be back about 4.30 see you soon, love you'.

I look at the time. It's 1 o'clock, so I got a few hours before they reach. My mum gonna be well pissed off when she gets home. The weather's been so bad it's wrecked the garden, that's my mum's pride and joy. The arches are broken, the climbing roses are all mashed up, my dad's gonna be vex, so much money went into it. I took some pictures and tried to tidy it, but trust me I don't have green fingers, well only for smoking!

'I always knew you and Kriss would end up together. What do you think your dad's gonna say?' Claire asks.

'I dunno, he's a bit funny like that. He'll most probably say summit like, well if that's wot she wants she's gonna do it, you make your bed you lie init, wotever that means, but I think he'll be OK. My mum loves Kriss off, she always has.'

'Yer, she always used to say stuff about him, she asked me a few times if he was single.'

'Wot, my mum?'

'Yer, she ain't easy. I told him though. He's always loved you, well as long as I can remember, but he didn't want to hurt you, the time weren't right he used to say. So I told him to leave you alone. He was a player, that's wot he done, who he was! Not no more though, he's changed.'

'Claire are you all right with everything?'

'Yer man, I love that I'm happy it's you. For a while I thought he was gonna do summit silly cause he believed you weren't interested. I'm so glad you gave him the chance to prove how he feels.'

'Me too. I do love him you know.'

'Yer, I know you do Jen. I can see how happy you both are.'

Kriss walks in with flowers and chocolates for mum and a bottle of French brandy for my dad.

'Look at you babe! You feeling a bit nervous?' I say with a chuckle, giving him a hug,

'A little darling, it's the dad bit, I've never had that! It's a bit hard babe.'

'You'll be all right, my dad's a big softy. When he meets you he'll know why I've fallen for ya, don't worry jus be yourself.'

Claire's laughing, saying she ain't ever seen Kriss like that. I roll him a spliff he's looking kinda pale! I try and put his mind at rest.

'Time's getting on we'll have to make a move soon.'

'What happened at Leona's?' he asks. I tell him about the train and wot the police said, he goes along with it. Claire's watching his reaction. He's cool and calm.

'Yer, I heard he owed someone money. Maybe he just had enough.

Well he weren't in a good place was he?' Claire's buying it. We can't afford to let anything slip.

Is that how it's done, just like that? I didn't want that, not like that. I feel like I'm up to my neck shit deep. If the truth ever came out I'm fucked! But the police said he jumped. I don't know wot to think any more.

'You ready babe?' I turn to look at him

'You all right babe?' he asks.

'Yer, just thinking.'

'About wot?'

I make up summit, don't wanna hot up the play in front of Claire.

'Yer, let's go.' They'll be getting home soon, that's one more thing. How am I gonna get through this like nuffin happened? We head to the car and get in. Kriss drives off and then he stops and parks up.

'Babe, wot's on your mind?'

So I tell him. 'I just wanted him hurt, look wot happened! Why are the police sayin he jumped in front of a train and now he's dead? Wot's going on, Kriss? Is he dead because of me?'

'Na babe' he says. 'Mackie got hold of him and gave him a right beating. There was some kinda chase or summit, that's when he jumped. I say jumped, I think he was just runnin away, didn't look and got hit. Like you said though, the police are saying that he jumped, so it all pans out just right.'

'Yer I know, but...'

'Na babe, no butts about it, wot's done is done. So is life, sometimes things happen not always the way they're meant to, but shit does happen and we have to deal with it. He can't hurt no one now.'

'Kriss, stop it.'

'Babe, don't worry, it's only us that know.'

We drive to mine. It's like 4.20 pm and they're not back yet. We go in, Kriss puts the flowers in the sink and the brandy on the side.

I'm gonna try not to think about it any more. The police are saying he did jump, that's good enough for me. We cuddle up on the sofa for a bit and have a kiss. That's brought me straight back to where I should be happy and loved up, that's wot it's all about.

Finally they're home

With that I hear a horn go. 'They're here' I shout. We go to the door together and look at each other. Kriss takes a deep breath.

I rub his arm and open the door. My mum's so happy to see me. The road's all tidy now, you would never know a boy lost his life out there a few days ago, apart from the little bits of police tape left on the lamp posts.

She's holding me tight and whispering in my ear 'Wot's going on.'

'I tell you inside mum' I say, kissing her. I go and hug my dad.

'Wot have you done?' he says.

'Nuffin.' I laugh. The twins are sleeping. I open the car door, I've missed them!

'Wake up, you're home' I say tickling them, they're pleased to see me.

'Jen I've missed you' Lucie says kissing me. 'And me' says Abbie, leaning over to hug me.

'I've missed you more' I say. 'Let's go in.'

We're all inside now. 'Mum, you know Kriss.' She grabs him for a kiss, you know how mothers are. I take Kriss by the hand. 'This is my dad, Peter.' They shake hands, I leave them to it.

My mum's on one, asking me stuff. She looks at me like she's gonna cry.

'Wot is it mum?'

'Your finger, what's that?'

'Nuffin' I say. She wasn't meant to see that!

'Mum, come in the front room a minute.' This is it, I'm gonna tell them now. I look for Kriss an dad, I see them in the garden talking. Well, Kriss is doing all the talking, my dad's just standing there straight faced. He's hard to read, that's where I get it from.

My mum walks in as I'm watching them.

'Wot are they doing? It's too cold to be out there. Wot's going on Jen?'

'Kriss asked me to marry him the other day.' It just came out. I should have worded it better!

'You're serious? You're too young.'

'Mum, you was with dad at the same age and you're still together happy and that, so wot's the difference between us?'

'You're pregnant?'

'No I'm not. We love each other mum, as simple as that, no more no less.'

'We'll see wot your dad's gonna say' she says with raised eyebrows.

'Mum, you know how I feel about him, he's everything I want all rolled into one.'

'Jen, how long has it been.'

'Since wot mum, how long wot?' Here we go.

'You an Kriss. Cos you two weren't together before we left for Bristol.'

'No, but we've wanted to be with each other for ages, and now we've finally made it and I'm not letting go. I love him mum!'

I walk towards the back door.

'Leave them to it Jen!' she says. 'Kriss needs to say his bit. He's a nice boy. Not sure how your dad's gonna take it though. You're his little girl, no matter how big you are. Dad knows Kriss is a good guy deep down. It will all work out darling.'

I feel her arms round me. She puts her head over my shoulder and says 'I always knew that you would end up with him. Does he make you happy, Jen?'

I turn around and face her, we're still holding each other. 'Mum, I love him, I really love him, I want to be with him. I'm the person I wanna be when I'm with him, he's good for me.'

'Then I'm happy for you darling. You gonna show me the ring then?'

I take my hand out of my tracky suit an she starts crying. 'Oh Jen it's gorgeous! When, ow, tell me everything.'

I tell her about the hotel and the love nest. She can't believe it.

'When your dad sees how happy you are he'll be fine, you know him already.'

'I hope so mum.'

The back door's open and Kriss walks in first, then my dad behind him, I'm looking to see what's going on. Kriss gives me one of his beautiful smiles so I know everything's kool.

My dad's like 'so you two are getting married?' I look at him, 'yer' I say and go and hug him, there really ain't any words for how I'm feeling. I go over to Kriss, he puts his arms round me. I love him so much. My mum welcomes him to the family and trust he's gonna need it. My dad's loving the brandy, he and Kriss are getting on like they've known each other for years. I'm liking it, but mum's feeling a bit left out until she sees the flowers and chocolates. I keep on catching my dad watching Kriss! They're so much alike in their own little ways, not to look at but wot they stand for (family is everything).

We stay a while. The twins are as loud as ever into stuff, digging round. One finds summit the other one wants, that's when all hell breaks loose.

I just come out with it. 'I'm gonna stay over Kriss's tonight.' I look at him but he's just doing his own thing. He believes I should be living at his, and to tell the truth I can't wait!

'OK darling I was hoping you would stay in tonight, but never mind when you come home tomorrow we can catch up' mum says. I feel bad now I've missed them all so much, and now I'm going.

My dad's telling Kriss about the drive home. He's always talking about summit, bless him. My mum's like 'oh shut up, he don't want to hear about road workings, he's a driver he knows already' and tilts her head backwards. I go and find the twins to say bye, they're in their room watching a dvd. I tell them I'll see them in the morning. Abbie's like 'wot, you going bed?' I laugh. 'No silly, I'm going out.'

'Where?' she asks. 'Up the road.' I say be good and leave them to it.

I go back downstairs. Mum's in the kitchen, my dad's talking to Kriss. They're really getting on, I knew they would. I go an hug my mum and tell her I love her and that I'll see her in the morning.

'Love you too' she says as I'm walking through to get Kriss. 'We're going now dad.'

'Oh, OK then, I'll see you soon mate' he says to Kriss, shaking his hand. Mum comes in to say bye to Kriss. She gives him a hug and a kiss on the cheek. 'See you soon' he says and we leave. We walk to the car, it's a bit up the road, Kriss grabs my hand, I love that feeling. He puts his arm round me.

'Wot was you talking to my dad about?'

'I just told him the truth.'

'Wot's that then?'

'I love you and I respect you and that's why I asked you to marry me.'

'Wot, just like that?'

'Yer, I thought I would just get in there with it. Wot could he really say, it's true?'

We get to the car and get in, it's kinda cold out there. I'm pleased it went well. We get back to Kriss's. I've got a bit of a headache and I go to lie down, Kriss has to go out bless him. He made me tea first. I'm lying here thinking about everything, how come people know each other but don't really know each other at all. Do you ever really know anyone? I mean you know wot they're telling you, what they want you to hear, but that's bullshit. I want to believe I know everything about

Kriss, but I don't think I know the half of it, I don't really want to. As long as he's safe and that he comes home to me, I don't think he would cheat or nuffin like that. I know nuff girls who would try a thing still.

He's up the road meeting who, going where, I don't know. It never used to bother me, I just saw him as some hot guy who I fancied that happened to be my mate's brother. I knew a bit about him, heard certain things, that's what drew me to him in the first place, but it's not about that now! All the nice things, the house the car and everything that goes with that, none of it would matter. I've fallen for him as a person. I love him and whatever comes with that I'll have to deal with.

My head's still working overtime. I shut my eyes and try to sleep. I lie there for about half an hour, just can't drift off so I get up to make a cuppa tea. Kriss ain't back yet, Claire's not in. I grab my drink and go and sit down, I look over at the clock, it's only 10.30. Feels like I've been sleeping for ages!

Sitting here waiting for I don't know wot, everything that's happened, it's all a madness. There's something I need to do.

It hurts

I grab my trainers and fling on my coat and hit the road. I go and check Delroy, see wot gawn with Maggie, so I'm there. We're smoking a joint, then one piece of gal comes in half-dressed. She's a fucking state, if you ever see her, nasty, I look at him.

'Wot you doing? We gotta find Maggie.'

'For wot? I don't want her here any more' he says.

'That's your daughter, she needs you right now. Claire saw her on road begging a change. I've heard other stuff as well.'

'She's hurt me too much. I don't wanna know any more.'

'She's on drugs Del.'

'Wot you saying? We all smoke Jen.'

'She ain't smoking weed, she's taking white [coke]. I'm scared for her, we have to do summit before it's too late. Yer all right she's a pratt sometimes, I've wanted to hurt her myself, she's fucked up, but we all need help sometimes and she needs us now.'

I talk him round and we leave. It's cold out here but he's got a little van so at least we don't have to walk.

My phone rings, its Kriss.

'Ello babe, I'll be home soon' he says.

'I'm not there darling.'

'Where are you babe?'

'Out looking for Maggie with her dad.'

He tells me not to be out there too long and he'll see me soon.

'OK babes, love you.'

'Love you too.' He hangs up.

We've been driving for a while an she's nowhere, I can see he's hurting. Well that's her dad, no matter wot she's done. We thought we saw her but it weren't. He still blames hisself for wot happened to her, that's why I think he'll prefer not to have her around, then he won't have to deal with it. But you can't do that, families should be there for one another. Don't matter wot that one person's done, blood is thicker than water, so they say.

We park up and sit for a bit hoping to see her, but we don't.

'If she doesn't want to be found she won't' he says. I know he's right but least were out here looking. Delroy carries on to say in the run up to her leaving they fell out.

'Why wot happened?' I ask him.

'She told me that she was into girls, that she don't like men in that way, but you know summit Jen, I knew.'

'So that's why she left.'

'Na Jen, I told her I was kool with it.'

'So wot then?'

'She said she was disgusted with herself and didn't understand why she was feeling that way.'

That's why I always used to see her with them dirty men, the really ruff ones, she would throw herself at anyone, the lowest of the bunch, men you wouldn't give a second look to, like she didn't care. It's all making sense now I think to myself, I can't tell her dad that though. We hang round for a bit but it's like looking for a needle in a haystack.

'I've gotta get home now Jen, can I drop you somewhere?'

'Yer, at the Hole in the Wall please.'

'Wot's that, Clapham?'

'Yer thanks, I'll jump on the bus, it takes me to the end of Kriss's road. You never know I might just get lucky and see her.'

144

I get the 88 to Vauxhall Park, no sight of her. I walk through and see Naz on the roadside.

'Jen can I talk to you?'

'Naz man, I'm not in the mood I'm tired' but he walks with me.

'Jen, I'm sorry for that thing, yer? You know what Claire's like.'

'Yer I do Naz and you know how I am, you shouldn't have even gone there, summit like that. You should have passed it by me first, you know I don't roll like that. If Kriss ever found out you'd be fucked, so wot was you thinking man?'

'I don't know Jen, she just kept on sayin you guys needed it so I sorted it ASAP, you know I got your back.'

'Claire is a bit pushy but you best know say next time run thing through me first, cos if not them man will fuck you up and that's your business get me?'

All he kept saying was 'I know man, I know'.

'Yer you best know' I say. 'Have you seen Maggie?'

'Na fam.'

'If you do let me know as soon as, kool.'

'Kool Jen we all right now.'

I've known him too long, he's lucky say I like him!

'Yer, just check yourself yer?'

'Nice one, I'll holla at you.'

I say later and we part ways. Kriss's is round the corner, I see his car and go and knock the door, he comes and lets me in.

'Ello babe, any joy?'

'Na she's nowhere to be seen' I say, kissing him.

'Do you wanna drink babe?'

'No thanks, can we just go to bed?'

I take him by the hand and lead him to the bedroom. I start undressing him and slowly kissing him. I want him so much. We lie down, I take my top off, his touch brings my body alive, I can't get enough of him skin to skin. I could kiss him all day long, we just fit. It's the best feeling ever. When someone loves you that much nuffin else matters, well not that I don't care about anyone or anything cos I love my family to death, but this love I'm feeling for Kriss, it's outa this world!

He's so gentle with me, taking his time, I like it.

'I love you' he says over and over. The pleasure he gives me, sometimes I have to check myself it's like it's a dream. How can this be happening to me?

He always makes sure I enjoy myself. He goes out of his way to please me and trust he does. He's so good in the sheets it's un-fucking-true. He's showing me a thing or two (I say with a smile).

I needed that, I think to myself. I'm so tired I close my eyes and drift, you know when you're half in half out of sleep, that's where I am feeling nice though.

Can't remember anything else well until I hear my phone ringing. I have a look at the screen, it's Sonia.

Back down the hospital

'Hello wot's up girl?'

'You need to come to the hospital.'

'Why wot's going on?'

'It's Shelly, she's lost the baby.'

'I'm on my way!' I leave Kriss sleeping and catch a cab, I know the driver so it's a free ride. When I get there Shelly's with the doctor, I'm hoping everything's all right, but it weren't. The baby's gone.

We all have a cry. The doc wants to make sure everything's come away, and she gets sent home with some painkillers and the all clear. We get her home, her parents are beside themselves and little Mark bless him, but there's nuffin none of us can do.

I make my excuses and leave. I just walk, it's hard to take in. I walk round the block like five times before heading back to Kriss's, I take off my coat and that. I'm freezing, it's so cold out there, I get back in bed and cuddle up to Kriss.

He made me laugh. 'Babe you're so cold' he says, half asleep. It come in like he's talking a different language, you know that sleep talk. He's funny, he ain't got a clue I've even been out, I'll tell him later.

I lie there in his arms. Knowing wot's happened a tear runs down my cheek on to Kriss, I hope we don't have to deal with summit like that I think, holding him tight! I know Jason is a waste man but that poor little baby we all ended up wanting, looking forward to meeting him or her. Bless Shelly, she wanted that baby! We'll have to be strong, be there for her you know.

I didn't really get to speak to Sonia, she was looking good though, I wonder wot's going on there.

I can hear the birds tweeting, it's getting light outside. Soon enough I fall asleep, not for long though. Sometimes I feel to just leave certain people behind, you know? I like to live my life to the max, do things, enjoy wot I have, appreciate it for wot it is, wot I can make it. I've got plans for my life. I don't wanna be someone just getting by, working all hours for stupid money, I see it every day. People struggling to make ends meet, I don't wanna end up like that, I'll do wotever it takes. I'm on the right road. Well, never say never, I understand things happen that we can't control, but life is wot you make it and I intend to make it a good 'un.

I get up, leave Kriss a note, *Couldn't sleep gone to see mum x love you* and head out the door. I know she'll be up, when we was little I remember mum used to wake us all up with her singing. Some high pitch shit. Always thought that birds and animals would follow her, you know like the cartoons on the telly, come in like how we used to have to sing in assembly at school! After last night I just need to see her, so much has happened, but I will keep it short and sweet.

I reach the house, there's mum on a chair cleaning the windows as usual.

'Hi luv' I say.

'Oh Jennie you didn't half make me jump' she says.

'Sorry mum, it's too early for all that.' I'm talking about the windows.

'Well I cooked dinner already. What you doing up an out darling?'

'Couldn't sleep, Shelly lost the baby last night.'

'Oh babes, come ere.' She gives me a cuddle, asking if she's OK.

'We were at the hospital late last night. Mum, it was so sad. She's at home now.'

We go in the house, I can hear my dad snoring. A bomb could land in our garden and dad would sleep though it, trust! That's why mum's up so early bless her. We go into the kitchen, mum makes tea, we have a chat about things. She made it clear certain things happen in life and there's nuffin we can do about it, we have to just get on with it and be there for Shelly.

'Things happen for a reason Jen, life is hard sometimes but we find a way and it makes us stronger, in time she'll be all right bless her. And how's Leona?'

I tell her about the court and what happened, and left it at that. She couldn't believe it, she's like 'Wot the fuck is this world coming too?'

I can see she wants to say something, and she does. 'Jen, are you sure about where your life's going? It's gonna be such hard work, you're only young.'

'I know mum, to tell you the truth I'd be lying if I said I wasn't scared, but it's not like we're getting married tomorrow. We both got things to do first. I'm wrapped up with college and Kriss understands that. We know it ain't gonna be easy but he loves me and we want to build a life together.'

'That's my girl, I had to make sure' she says with a smile.

'You are funny' I say, hugging her. 'He's asked me to move in with him mum, how would you feel about that?'

Mum says nothing for a few moments and then 'We just want you to be happy darling, and I can see by the way you talk about him, my little girl all grown up.'

'It's not far mum, I'll bring you round soon.'

Feeling a bit sleepy I go and lie down in my room. Lying there on the bed it feels like I've outgrown the space. Growing up I never had my own room, always had to share, never any time for myself. I'm one of them people who loves their own company. Sometimes I need to be on my own too, reflect on things, that's when things start to make sense, fall into place. I've always been an observer, stand back, listen, get the full picture of what's going down and the way my life is heading. Right now I'm loving it. Can't wait to be Mrs Campbell - that sounds funny, I'll have to get used to that one.

I fell asleep and had a well weird dream, I'd lost summit, don't know what, but I couldn't find it nowhere. When I woke all I wanted to do was be with Kriss. I really love him, he means everything to me, the love gets stronger every day. When I see him it's like the first day I ever saw him, even now he takes my breath away.

I jump in the bath, get dress and phone Kriss, he picks up.

'Ello darling, where's you?'

'At my mum's. And you?'

'At home waiting for you' he says.

'I'm on my way darling, won't be long.' I hang up. 'Mum I'm making a move now, love you.'

'Love you too. Are we gonna see you later Jen?'

'Not sure mum.' I kiss her and leave.

I reach Kriss's and let him know about Shelly. We have a cuddle.

'Jen' he says holding me, 'You been through so much with everyone's troubles babe, it's time to let go of them people, you can't look after them any more. It's time to start looking after yourself babe.'

I just stand there holding him, crying, cos I know he's right but I love them. I think to myself, Kriss doesn't let anyone in, so when summit happens he's detached from the pain that comes with everyday life. After losing his mum he changed. Not that he doesn't care, he just keeps everyone at arm's length, thankfully not me though.

He wipes away my tears. 'Babe, I would never keep you away from your friends, you know that don't ya?'

'Yer of course' I say, but it doesn't make it any easier.

Life is a lesson

'We all have to learn to stand on our own two feet. It's hard, but we just get on with things.'

Bless him! I understand wot he's saying, it's time for us to grow up and not lean on each other so much, but that don't stop me from caring any less. They'll always be my girls.

'Let's go for a drive' Kriss says. 'I need to get away for a bit.'

'Where though?' I say.

'Let's just get in the car and drive.'

So that's wot we done. We ended up in Brighton and walked along the sea front, its bloody cold, we must be mad! Hugging each other like human windbreaks. We found a little coffee shop, proper old fashioned, warm and inviting. We had a pot of tea and some London cake with custard. It's just nice to get away from all the madness.

Kriss amazes me every day. It's like he can read me so well, that's what it's all about, finding that special someone to share your life with. If you're lucky enough you find that one person and that's it for the rest of your life.

We finish up and leave, it starts to rain. We try and get back to the car but we've walked a fair bit. We see a shelter and head over there. We're soaked through. We try to keep each other warm, well it got a bit steamy under there let me tell ya, fucking hell I can't help myself

I'm all over him like a rash. The more I'm with him the more I want him. I've heard stories about people in love, but that's nothing like wot I'm feeling. It's more much more intense!

We see a hotel and go in out of the rain. I'm feeling a little naughty and Kriss has that look in his eye so we book a room and head upstairs, still dripping wet. We get to the room and shut the door behind us.

What a time we had, shit, swear down it's like an outta body experience (wow!) he takes me to a place I've never been. The way he makes me feel it's priceless! He whispers in my ear 'Why did it take us so long?'

I kiss him, we're all hot and sweaty. I look into his eyes.

'I love you' I say, and I so meant it with all of me. The way I am when I with him I can be myself, nothing and no one else matters. That sounds bad but it's the truth.

'I wanted this, you, for so long' I say 'and now I've got you there's no letting go. You're stuck with me.'

He holds me tight. 'I hope so, that's all I want' he says. We lie there in each other's arms.

We stay the night and leave early in the morning. Kriss has a big job on today, I don't like to know really! As long as he's safe and comes back in one piece. The people he deals with, they've all been working together a long time so they've built up a good trust level. They bring things in, then it's Kriss's job to delegate. If it weren't for Kriss all them mans on road wouldn't be in business, so it's not like anyone would even try and step to him, that's when everything would go a bit nuts. The guys he works with, trust they're not easy at all, and the police, there's nothing they can really do, he's never round drugs or anything so they could pull him all day long. Trust me he's not just a pretty face. When you're at the top of your game and you play it fair there's no need for you to dirty your hands, you pass that shit down! We get home, Kriss has to go.

'Stay safe babe' I say, kissing him. 'Love you' he says.

Kriss drives off I go in and head to bed. I've come up with a plan. If I go to sleep when I wake up he'll be back, so that's wot I do. I slept a good few hours, got a couple of missed calls, nuffin from Kriss, then a text comes through, *Love you babe see you soon darlin just finishing up xx*

Sent one back, *Love you to darling come on then xxxx*

I can't wait for him to get here, I hate it when I can't see him. My mind works overtime, I get these images. My imagination is off the scale sometimes, I scare myself. Everything could be fine, but I build up a string of pictures in my head and I add to it, then that's it, the worst thing has happened. But it's all in my head so I can't feel safe until I see him. It's cos I know wot he does, I know the danger. I hate that feeling but you know you fall for the person knowing everything, I'll have to get used to it! That's what he does, hopefully not for long, he's never done anything else, that's all he knows.

I hear him outside, I'm so relieved he's OK. He walks in and flings his arms around me. 'Ello darling.' He kisses me and tells me about his day, not in depth.

Claire phones, she's staying out tonight. I think she's got a new man.

'Baby do you wanna go out and eat?' he says.

'Na, can we stay in?'

He looks at me. 'That's wot I love about you.' He smiles.

'Wot do you mean?'

'It's not the money with you' he says, unsure of the situation.

It's never been like that for me, I roll deeper than that. Yes, money makes the world go round but not everyone is out for wot they can get. Money can make ya or break ya but it can't buy you happiness. Fair dos it can buy you nice things, but nice things don't make the person, it's the person that makes the person, if you get me!

We smoke a bit, have a little drink, I'm feeling nice. He's telling me how good we've got it, wot he made today most people don't make in a lifetime, an that's just one day! But I don't business bout that, money

153

don't rule me. Kriss carries on to say the meeting that took place today only happens four times a year, cos of the quantity and quality of the ting. That makes me feel a whole heap better. I don't really know nuffin about them things, I just smoke weed, I'm not into nuffin else, I've seen wot crack can do and brown's no better.

'Babe' he says 'I won't be doing this for much longer'. I hope not, but I fell for him knowing wot he done and to tell the truth I wouldn't change him for nuffin.

He takes off his jacket and goes and pours a drink and hands it to me.

There's blood on his sleeve and his hands have cuts along the knuckles, like he's been fighting.

'Babe wot happened, your hands are bleeding?'

He looks at me a bit shady and says 'One of the mans didn't have the right peas (that's money) so I had to deal with the situation, but I'm all right babe.'

I keep on telling myself I know what he's about, what he does, so it shouldn't have me all shocked. I go an grab some cotton wool and salty water and clean them the best I can. We drink some more, Kriss starts to open up.

'I had to teach him a lesson.'

I don't really wanna hear it but I can see he wants to get it off his chest.

'Babe he's been late a few times now and the boys weren't having it. I just done wot had to been done, otherwise he'd be finished right about now.'

Fucking hell, this is really how they roll. Be careful wot you wish for, you know. Cos you never know wot it entails. There's two sides to every coin and every right has its wrong.

Now I understand wot my dad means - you make your bed you lie in it - and I have, so here we go!

It scares me what he's involved in. Before I just used to see him for who he was and now my wanting has turned to worry. When we're together I couldn't be happier, I feel whole, I can't get enough of him, but when he's out doing his thing I'm not in control any more and that's wot scares me, knowing anything can happen at any time. He has got a good network of people around him, but when it comes to it you're on your own, that is the way it is, that's how I see it. You can't trust anyone to have your back.

I've been there, I got stabbed up and them mans I was with were on their fucking toes! Big mans and little me, the worst thing was it had shit to do with me, I was at the wrong place at the wrong time, that's why you see me yer? I know people but I'd rather move on my own. I might be a young girl but trust me I've got bigger balls than nuff mans outta road. Kriss has got his head screwed on but it's that network of people? I met that guy Mackie, he seemed nice, well maybe that's the wrong word to use but I see he checks for Kriss and he'll do anything for him. Kriss is in the bath, my phone rings, it's Stacey.

'You all right luv?' I say. 'Yer babe, you? Can you talk?'

'Yer, go on.'

She starts by saying that she would rather see me to talk, but I weren't really feeling that, I just said I was out of London, but it was OK to chat.

'Jen, that little bitch set my brother up.' She's crying!

'Wot?' I try and calm her down so she can tell me wot she's saying.

'When Arron broke up with Lisa she swore down she would get him back and she did, but I thought she meant get back with him. She got her brother to do it. She was fucking there Jen, she watched him die.'

'Wot, how do you know this?'

'The police came round the house to say her brother was caught on CCTV and they could place Lisa there on her brother's say so. They've got the jacket one of them was wearing and it belongs to her, her DNA all over it and Arron's blood. The bitch!'

'Fucking hell Stacey, so wot's happening now?'

She carries on saying they've released the body and the funeral's on Saturday the 27th of November, 11.30 at St Anne's in Vauxhall, could I make it?

'Yer Stacey I'll be there, babe I've gotta go, sorry.'

I made it seem like I was out and about, didn't want to come across as heartless. We say our byes and I hang up. I do feel bad for them but there's nuffin I can do. It's nuffin to do with me and anyway the police have them now. Bloody heck, wot was I just saying? Now look, it's the people closest to you that will fuck you up in the long run (eyes wide open).

We're not kids no more

I go in the bedroom and lie down. A little while later Kriss comes in and jumps on me all playfully with just a towel on, he looks like one of them guys that model. He pins me down and starts kissing me. I'm not really in the mood but I go with the flow. I love the way I feel about this boy, nuffin comes close. He's worth his weight in gold.

We have a cuddle, I tell him about Stacey. I wanna be up front with him. He's so sweet, he said he would come with me, that's wot I wanted to hear.

I feel shattered. Kriss is in the kitchen making something to eat, I must have fallen asleep. I remember Kriss trying to wake me.

When I finally got up I could hear voices in the front room. I wasn't sure if I should go in there so I stayed where I was, brain's ticking, I think the worst! I can't help it, the way things have been lately it's like I've prepared myself for summit horrible to take place.

I couldn't take it no more. I walked in there after all that its Kriss and Jay smoking, just chilling.

'Ello darling' he says. I go and sit with him a minute, saying hi to Jay.

'Where's Claire?' I ask.

'She's seeing some guy.' They're laughing. 'Stop fucking about, where is she?'

'Na for true, she is seeing someone.'

I have a think to myself, wondering who it is. Jay's lookin at me a bit funny. She's not back with that waste man Deano? He's a total dickhead, he was just using her. I can't tell Kriss that though. He would fuck him up, no joke.

Then Kriss says summit that shocks me. 'I warned her, so it's down to her now.'

'Don't' I say, but trust, I think say he's had enough of her. She does go on a bit and if she don't get her own way she won't feel on way to try an diss you, but that's just her. She's always been able to twist Kriss round her little finger, but she's forgetting that we're all big people now and we're all taking different paths. It's time to grow up, we'll see!

Jay's saying there's one house party tonight and that we should reach, but I ain't feeling that.

'Babe, you go enjoy yourself' I say. Kriss is like 'Na, if you ain't going there's no point, it's all about us babe.'

That put a smile on my face. Jay looks at Kriss. 'Is that how you're goin on bruv?'

'Yer, it's like that. See this girl, she makes me want better for myself. She's my choice.' I look at Jay, by the look on his face he can see Kriss ain't fucking around.

'Na bruv, I'm joking I know how you feel about Jen.'

Kriss ain't having it. 'Jay listen, I ave ta bring you in on summit bruv, I love this girl ya undastand, no joke. Things are gonna change, she come first, get me?'

Kriss is sitting there elbows on his knees rubbing his hands together, he's making me a bit nervous. The look on his face he ain't ramping, he ain't easy. Wot could Jay really say? He feels like he's losing his boy, but he's not.

'Babes go out, its kool, I'm tired anyway.' He reaches over. 'Na it's been a long day I'm not feeling it.'

Jay's rolling a joint, I can see he's pissed off. I kiss Kriss.

'I'm going to lie down, later Jay.' He gets up and gives me a kiss on the cheek.

158

'Nite Jen, see you next time.' I turn to walk and as I pass Kriss holds his hand out, we touch just in passing. He gives me a cheeky wink.

I'm in the bedroom, I can hear them. Well, I can hear Kriss.

'I'm marrying her, get used to it, things ain't the same no more bruv.'

Jay's like 'Yer I understand, but them other girls you weren't like that, I'm not getting it bruv.'

'Listen, see them girls, they're nuffin, they don't mean shit, they're any time girls. I don't want that, I never did, they was just there. It's all about that girl in there, trust me this is deep shit bruv, she comes first and that's no lie. But we kool though.'

'I hear you' Jay said, 'every time bruv.' I didn't hear anything else cos I fell asleep (tut).

I wake up to soft kisses all over my body. He's had a drink, god knows how many spliffs they smoked. He's so gentle, kissing my face, looking at me.

'I love you' he says, holding me. 'Babe, I'm sorry about earlier but he knows this is it for me, and the mans, them are gonna ave to get used to not aving me around so much.'

But I know he can't jus walk away from them tings, he's built up a rep for himself, I understand more than he thinks. When your wrapped up in them things it's hard to get out and wot makes it worst, he's good at wot he does (it's fuckin hard). I just want him to be happy. Kriss wants to start making plans but I've got a few things to sort first, I can't go into married life with certain things hanging over me.

I hold him close until I fall asleep. I love the way he makes me feel. Safe.

I had a wicked sleep, now I know he's in it for the long term.

All at once

Kriss is up and dressed! 'Babe where you off too?' I say as I shuffle up to sit, combing my hair with my fingers.

'I told you babes. I've got this thing going on with Phil, we're looking at a few bars today.'

'Oh yer sorry lover.' He's like do I wanna tag along, they're going a little out of London. 'Come babe, we can grab some lunch and make a day of it?' But I'm not gonna go, I've got my own tings on today.

Kriss looks so sexy in a suit, I want him to come back to bed! But he's gotta go now, wot a shame. As he leaves he turns and says 'look out for the post babe' and blows me a kiss.

I get up and run a bath. I'm gonna try and sort out everything one time. On a mission today?

I must have been in there a good half hour, then I hear the door. I get out and wrap a towel around myself and go to see who it is. I pop my head around the door, some guy saying can I sign? So I did, it's my name on the document. He hands me wot I don't know. I go in wondering do I open it? Na, I'll phone Kriss.

'Babe sorry, but something came to the house, it's got my name on it?' I feel a bit stupid.

'Yer it's for you darling, open it, have a read. I've gotta go baby, love you.'

'Love you too.'

I put it on the table, it's like an A4 brown envelope, fuck knows! I go and make tea and light a fag ,yes a fag, it's a bit too early for a joint even though I could do with one. I sit down at the table and finish smoking, wondering what it could be, so I pick it up and tear the strip off. I'm a bit nervous, you know that sickie feeling.

'Oh come on Jen' I say out loud, so I do it. I put my hand in and pull out some paperwork. Wot? I turn it round and there it is, the papers for the love nest. Shit!

I'm looking at it and where it says 'owner' it says 'Jennie Richards', that's me, shit its mine it's all mine! I thought I was going in 50/50, Kriss said he'd bought into it. I wasn't expecting that one. There's no question that the boy loves me, he's got a saying, if you think it say it, and if you want something, go get it.

I had to send him a text, *Wot have you done, I love you so much xx* That's all I can do, I ain't got no money, all I got to give is me!

I don't really understand wot the papers mean. I put them back in the envelope and put them in a drawer in Kriss's room.

I go and fix up ready to step out. my heads still in a spin. I've proper landed on my feet with Kriss but trust I'm gonna put the graft in. That's why I've been working hard at college to get the grades to hopefully build a good life for myself. Chef has only good things to say about me. If he wants something showing to the class or to take change of the class that's right, he'll put me up!

To be able to grow, achieve certain things in the industry which I have grown to love.

En route to Leona's

I need to know wot's been said about Marcus. I'm not really a phone person, text yes, but I prefer to talk face to face, see people's expressions. Their actions speaks volumes. All this walking, my bloody leg's hurting!

I get to the house and knock the door, Leona answers it.

'Wah gawn g' I say, trying to keep things real.

We go through to the front room. I don't know why we call it that cos it's at the back of the house.

'So wot you been up to girl?' She puts the kettle on.

'Well just to let you know it was Marcus.'

She goes kinda quiet.

'OK, so wot then?' I ask.

'It's like no one understands, I loved him Jen.'

Wot, is this bitch crazy?

'Are you fucking dumb, he nearly killed you fam! You're a fucking fool!'

She's all crying up the place, just looking at her she's making me feel sick.

'Wot's bloody wrong with you?' I had to tell her about herself.

'You know summit Leona, just do wot you're doing yer, and fucking grow up!'

Then I just got up and walked out. I need to get away from her!

I don't wanna hear that shit after how he treated her. She's got time and wot's the point he's fucking dead. It's not like she can go round an sort things out! I mean who in their right mind would?

I'm not on that, from when their saying he jumped I'm not holding no guilt. He was a fucking waste man! No good for nuffin, not sayin' that he deserved to die, but wot goes around comes around. She needs to see that or I don't wanna know any more. I've got my own shit to deal with, I can't keep picking up after everyone else, not no more.

Things to do, places to go

How the hell did it come to this? she pissed me right off. She's gonna do wot she wants, can't be round that.

Walking up the road to go check Shelly, a car pulls alongside me. I'm having a good look and see Claire. 'Wah gawn fam?' I say. She's like 'jump in'. Some yout is driving.

'So wot's good Claire, where you been?' I see her hand on the brother's knee.

'You know how it is Jen.' Watch her na. 'B this is my sister in-law.'

I look in the rear view, he's all watching me hard, like we slept together or summit, dirty little shit, Claire's so lovely, she can do so much better.

I didn't say nuffin, just carried on talking to her, she said she's coming home later so we'll catch up then. I give her a kiss and make tracks. I don't know wot she sees in them mans, I'll talk to her later.

Anyway that was handy bumping into her, that's number two on my list done. I'm looking forward to spending a bit of time with her, not sure about wot's his name but we'll see init?

As I'm walking I can hear loud voices coming from one of the little shops, I have a look in. Some guy has hold of someone, shouting 'You fucking little thief' and sayin he's gonna phone the old bill. As he swings the person round it's only fucking Maggie, if you ever see her!

164

I feel ashamed to even say I know her, but that don't stop me from trying. I go in, say 'what's happening? I know her, wot's she done?'

He's looking kinda pissed, you can't blame him, she been nicking stuff. He's got the phone in his hand.

'Hold up bruv, I beg you don't phone the police, how much is it?'

He's cussing bout he don't want the food back, that he can't sell that now.

'So how much?' I ask. He's like '£7.49'.

'Well can I just pay for it? She won't come in here again.'

So anyway he lets me pay.

Outside I phone Delroy but he don't wanna know (he's telling me she's dead to him). I understand, family push and push and sometimes people can't forgive or forget, well he doesn't see that he done anything wrong.

I can't take her to Kriss's but I wouldn't do that anyway, maybe Leona can help. It would be good for her, keep her busy. I phone her, she kool for her to be there, they've always sort of been there for each other, so it's a good thing. I walk her round there, ain't no point in talking to her, she ain't with it and to make matters worse she looks a fucking state. She stinks. I didn't go in, just left them to it.

Back on track

Feel a bit hungry, so I pop in the café and take a seat. Sid comes over and takes my order.

'How are you?' he says 'Long time I ain't seen you and the girls, how is everyone?' I show him my ring, he's funny. 'But you're too young, if you was my daughter, well.' I don't think so!

I had to laugh, he can't bloody talk, has been married like five times, so wot don't work for one may work for another, and it's how you as a couple treat each other.

He takes the weight off and then starts telling me things ain't been too good. His wife ran off with the pot wash man, and they come in everyday and don't pay, wot a ting, thinking to myself, that's how people stay out for wot they can get!

Sid's like 70 goin on 30, he's really sweet, takes pride in himself and the café is doing well, everyone comes here. He sells anything from egg and chips to jerk chicken. Wot can I say, I just want my food, my belly's hungry.

Trust me I understand where he's comin from, if wants me to talk to them kool, cos trust, when I say they won't be back (wankers), how fucking dare they.

Nice, here comes my food, beans on toast with bacon and a lovely cuppa.

'Thanks Sid.'

It's nice and warm in ere, a couple of old dears in the corner drinking tea bless em. My phone rings, I answer it. 'Ello mum.'

'Ello darling, why haven't I seen you, I can't remember wot you look like.'

My mum's funny, I do miss her. 'I'm just eating, where are you lovely girl?'

'At home, you coming?' she asks.

'Yer mum, give me 20 minutes, I've got some juice for ya.'

She wants me to tell her over the phone, but I won't, she'll have to wait for that one. We say bye and I finish my food, take my plate an cup to the counter ready to pay.

'Sid, wot do I owe ya?' he's shaking his head. I leave a fiver on the till, watch him.

'You're too bad' he says, kissing his teeth.

'We all need to make a living Sid, stop giving food away' I tell him. I'll see him soon, he's happy for that (and I will pop in, he's a nice old man).

Some people take the piss cos they can, Sid don't have no family never had kids or nuffin, but us lot have known him as long as I can remember. When I was about 11 mum used to bring us ere. I swear down wot I'm gonna say next is so true, my mum is the only person I know that eats a burger in a bun with a knife and fork (no joke) but I won't have her any other way.

I've done some proper fucked up things over the years nuff, parents would have gave up (just like Delroy with Maggie). Well I never done hard drugs, I've known people on it, but me, na. Still I was pretty fucked up doing all sorts, spending other people's money.

You know one time me and my sisters went up West End, it was wicked. We got nuff stuff. The funny thing about that day was we were in one shop and Marie was buying some clothes an she had to sign for it, but Marie as she is only wrote her real name and gave it to the lady. She pull Marie and said the card and the name she signed were different. Marie was so quick on it an said, 'oh I changed my name by deed poll a few weeks ago, you wouldn't believe how many times I've done that'. The lady just went with it and put it through, we shopped all day!

On my way to mums

I get there an I don't even have my keys, I have to ring the bell like everyone else (a bit strange) but still, I can hear my mum cussing my dad to get up. She opens the door.

'Hello luv' she says, arms out for a hug. 'Where's your keys?'

'At Kriss's wot you cussing about?' Like I don't know!

'Your fucking dad, he's lazy.' Wot's she like!

'Mum man, did he go work last night?'

'Yer he got in about 5.30, cuppa tea?' I follow her to the kitchen.

'Oh, I've got something for you.' She goes through to the front room, she's only a few minutes. As she's heading back she's like

'Shut your eyes and hold your hands out' so that's wot I do. 'Open them' she says. It's a proper set of chef knives in a black case.

'Thanks mum, I love them!' They're wicked, each one is made from one piece of steel, that's the blade and the handle, and the weight of them so light.

'So they all right Jen?' mum says with a smile

'I love them, thanks' I say, kissing her.

Mum makes tea and we go and sit down. 'So where you been, wot you been up to?'

I tell her about Leona, then about Maggie an wot just happened.

'Bloody heck Jen, wot's wrong with everyone?'

She asks me about Kriss, I go on to tell her about this morning.

'Oh my god I need a fag' she says an sits down.

'Mum you can't tell no one, not even dad.'

She looks at me. 'Why not? What ain't you telling me?'

I walk over to the window an say 'I don't want people round here talking, it's just easier to keep things on the down.'

Mum starts drinking her tea. 'But Jen, why can't dad know?'

My brain works different to other people; I really do think the worst every time

'I just want to hold it down mum. I haven't even read it or talked to Kriss. I need time to get my head round it all.'

So I'm hoping that she keeps it to herself. That's my mum, I know she will.

'Ain't you got some of your stuff?'

She means weed. My parents know I smoke, it's my choice, I don't do nuffin else really, I go out once in a blue moon, it's not my thing, I'd rather stay in. I curl up on the sofa. It feels good to be home. Mum puts a blanket over me (I'm missing Kriss). It feels like I haven't seen him for ages, but it was only this morning (wot am I like!)

My eyes are closed but I can hear mum saying 'I'll phone Kriss to come over for his dinner, wot do you think Jen?'

'Na he's outta London on business mum, another night maybe.'

He's itching to be part of the family, but he don't realise he's in it already, he don't know wot he's let himself in for!

When we was younger I remember one day, my dad come home so drunk he was useless. We ended up nailing him to the floor and sewing up his flies (mum and me), it was so funny. That's what you get living with a house full of girls (bless him). We put make-up on him and sent him out to work, wot people must have thought when they saw him. He used to come home pissing himself with laughter, they were the good old days! When did everything turn so serious?

People work hard all their life, I see it in my parents. My dad's out

170

all hours and for wot? Yer he's all right but things could be better. Some wanker smashed his window, next one tried to rob him, the worst thing is my dad's a big fucking geezer, no joke.

That's wot I'm sayin, the streets ain't the place to be, mans getting shot dead gone. Next mans stabbed to death, missin, wot the fuck, girls are setting mans up to die. It come in like we all went to sleep and woke up in a movie, but there's no stop or pause, it's just rolling out one thing after the next, not knowing wot tomorrow holds.

'Where's the girls?' I ask. 'Oh they're over Martha's, it's her birthday.' Martha is one of them girls. She's so ugly she's cute, nuffin you do would help her but she's sweet though.

'Wot time does it finish mum, I'll pick them up?' Mum's putting the kettle on.

'Na you're all right Jen luv, I'm getting them about eight.' Wow that's a long one, when we were small they used to last an hour or so, by then parents had enough.

Mums like 'you rest darling, try an have a little sleep.' I can hear her pottering about, then nuffin. I was having a nice kip until I heard the little rats. Shit, look at the time, bloody heck.

'Do you want tea Jennie?' I sit up and get the girls to come and sit with me.

'I've missed you two.' I give them both a kiss, they're telling me about the party at the same time. I can't make out wot their saying, and they're getting louder. Mum tells them to go and get in their night stuff.

'Jennie, tea?'

Oh yer, yes please.' She makes it, then comes an sits with me.

'I've gotta go soon mum.' She offers me a fag.

'When am I gonna see you?' she asks. I'll have to bring them round soon, Kriss said anytime!

'I know mum' I say, holding her hand, we're used to seeing each other every day but now it feels like there's not enough hours in the day. I text Kriss to see wot time he's due back, get one back, *On way back, don't cook nuffin, I grab a Chinese on the way xxx* He'll be a good few hours.

'You gonna stay and have something to eat?' mum asks.

'No thanks, Kriss is picking up something on his way back. He's gonna wanna talk about the papers mum, but I don't want to, not tonight anyway, it's a bit out of my comfort zone. I don't wanna come across thick or nothing.'

'Wot you talking about? You're young, we all have to start somewhere. Kriss ain't gonna hold nothing against you.' She goes a bit deeper. 'He knows you're in college, wot your building towards. He's just cut out the middle man. College is gonna give you the foundation to grow and achieve the things you want darling, once you're there you'll pick up things quickly.'

I look at her like if to say, yer right. 'You will babe, you'll see' she says, giving me a cuddle. 'It will all work out Jennie.'

I love my parents so much, trust me I have fucked up in my time but I don't wanna be that hard head any more, I just want them to be proud of me. Yer OK I've been shifted (arrested) a good few times for all sorts of things, but I'm trying to put that life behind me. As for Kriss, no one round here really knows wot he does for a living, only the top geezers in the firm know who's in. On road mans know of him, but not wot he's about. No one gets close enough to hurt him because they don't really know, all they see is him out and about in a suit like some pen pusher. Kriss moves within a tight network of people on a need to know basis.

Still, I worry all the time, cos I know.

He's told me he wants out, but will it happen? I don't know, he's in deep, you know something, I never worry about him getting nicked, that's the last thing on my mind. It's all the other stuff that freaks me out.

I get up and go to the toilet. When I come out I ask mum where dad was.

'He's gone work' she says.

'Oh, I didn't see him.' He must have left when I was sleeping.

'You off now babe?'

I grab my coat. 'Yer.' I go and kiss her and have a little cuddle, then make a move.

Fucked up big time

I reach Kriss's, Claire's in music on weeds in the air. 'Hi Jen.' She's been in for a while by the state of her (she's lean up) let me just make some tea, it's cold out there. We end up in her room smoking, chatting. She's telling me about that guy, where she met him, that he's from Peckham, she knows he's a waste man and that she's in it for the sex. She got fucking time errrrr!

'Wot you on man, why can't you just find a nice guy?' She's rolling her eyes at me (she's too fucking rude). 'I know wot I'm doing' she says.

'You know your brother's on his way? You need to fix up, he don't wanna hear that!'

I wonder if she's doing it because she feels pushed out, so I ask her.

'Is this cos of me being with Kriss?'

She looks at me. 'Na babe, it's about me, I'm just having a bit of fun.'

I go over and turn down the music.

'Watch where fun takes you yer' I tell her.

I'm not even joking, she's making me feel a bit sick, about sex is she kidding me or wot! I thought she was better than that? Obviously not.

I go and run myself a bath, I've just had enough now. It come in like everyone just wants to fuck around no one wants to grow up, but you know you have to move with the times.

In the bath chilling

I hear the door go hoping its Kriss, I call out but there's no answer, then I hear swearing. I jump out. Kriss and Claire are going for it. I do understand where he's coming from.

'Get out you little bitch!' he says. She's crying.

'Don't fucking worry, I'm out of ere and I won't be back.'

'Claire man' I say.

'Na Jen I've had it, you're welcome to him man.'

'Baby' I say 'wot happened?' putting my arms around him.

'She took my mum's rings and sold them, I'll never get them back. That's a bit of her I wanted to hand down one day to our kids.'

I can see how upset he is. I go comfort him some more. Even I know you don't do them things, that's fucking low.

'I told you Jen, she's on her own now.' He's hurting. I know he doesn't mean it.

Kriss is in the kitchen plating up some food. I go in and join him and try to clear the air.

'How was today babe, see anything nice?' he hands me my food, it looks yummy.

'There was a few that stood out, really nice' he says, passing me a drink.

'So wot's your next move?' The food is so good.

'Phil wants to put an offer in. I'm gonna put some money in babe, trying to get my shit together. I know I have to start flying straight.' He holds my hand. 'Everything's coming together nicely.'

We finish up eating. 'My mum wanted you to come over for your dinner earlier.'

He looks at me. 'Bless her, we'll go soon, and they still haven't been here, wot about Sunday? Get them over ere.'

'Yer that would be nice, once my dad comes ere he won't wanna leave all them years with a house full of girls. He's gonna be in his element trust me, we won't be able to get rid of him.'

Kriss starts laughing. I love it when he's like that. He goes an jumps in the shower.

I do the washing up, can't get Claire out of my head. I'm hoping she'll tell me who's got the jewellery so I can get it back. Them things mean so much to Kriss, well it's the last link to his mum. She's so out of order! I'm really hoping that she borrowed money against them and put them in the pawn shop. I'll talk to her tomorrow.

If she needed money Kriss would have give her so I don't get, why would she wanna hurt him like that? It don't make no sense, unless she's on something?

Kriss comes out of the bathroom dripping wet, scoops me up and starts kissing me. 'I've been waiting to do that all day' he says, He carries me to the bedroom, I don't know where that come from, I feel like a naughty school kid behind the bike shed (not that I was ever behind it in the first place) maybe smoking weed! Before Kriss, I was a floater, not knowing where I was going, not knowing who I really was. Yer I'm in college doing my ting though. He's kinda fast tracked my life, but even if it weren't so, I would still be here. I've never met anyone like him, special. He takes me somewhere I want to be. The way he's touching me right now. I've always held something back, not no more, he's running his hands all over my body.

'I want you' he says softly. He starts kissing me slowly.

'You've got me' I say, looking into his eyes.

We take our time. You know when something works you just can't get enough? If Kriss was food I would be obese. If he was a drug I would be an addict, as simple as that. He's got me up, that's the way I like it.

He rolls a joint as we're smoking, kisses the top on my head.

'Them papers babe, we'll go through them tomorrow and you can sign them.'

I sit up on the bed cross-legged like a kid.

'Why did you do that babe?' I say.

'Wot darling?' passing me the joint.

'I don't understand, them papers have my name on it.'

'Did you get to look at them babe?' he said all seriously.

'Not really, I had a quick look, then I got a bit scared and put them in your drawer.'

He's smiling at me. 'Wot?' I say, giggling.

'It's all yours, sweetheart.'

I start crying. 'I can't do it. I don't know nuffin about running a place like that.'

He wipes my tears away. 'Karl's there, use him darling, soak up everything. Before you know it you'll be able to do it with your eyes shut babes.' He takes everything with a pinch of salt! His motto is, if you don't know something go suss it out. How can I ever thank him for being him!

So he's telling me about the layout of the places. The pictures are lovely, really nice, a bit far out, but it's a different kinda clientele they're hoping to pull in.

'It's got a kitchen. I was hoping you could set up a menu, put your stamp on the place. Wot do you think?'

'Yer why not?' It's like all this is happening to someone else.

He must be well knackered, bless him. He's got a heart of pure gold. We stay in bed and fall asleep.

I get up bright and early to try and catch Claire. I need to find this stuff. See wah gawn with this girl (she's fucked up big time, I don't know wot do her).

Kriss has done everything for her. He's had to proper fight for her, so it's like a kick in the teeth, you know wot I mean?

I try to ring her, its ringing.

'Hello?' She sounds messed up. 'Claire its Jen, I need you to meet me down the cafe now, yer?'

'Wot now?' she says. She gonna come, at least that's something I can work with. I go and jump in the shower. Sid will make me a nice cuppa, I think to myself. I fling on a tracky and head over, hoping she shows.

Down the café

Sid's made me some food, sweet dumplings, eggs and beans and tea. It's busy in here this time of morning, construction workers mainly.

The door opens, it's Claire. I feel to rip her face off but that ain't gonna get the things back. I have to hold it down.

She comes over. 'Jen don't start, yer?'

Is she taking the piss? This is all her doing. She sits down.

'Where is it?' I ask her. She won't look me in the eye.

'We've been through too much for things to end like this' I tell her.

'I needed the money Jen.' She thinks I don't know but Kriss tells me everything, he gives her 2 grand a month, tax free, shit that's 24 grand a year. For wot? For her to shit all over her brother.

I had to ask her a good few times. In the end she told me it was in the shop.

'How much?'

She starts crying, but you know I don't even want to hear it. She hands me the slip an I take a look, £650. I look at her and ask her 'wot was the point? Your brother done everything for you!' I'm so vex right now, I just don't understand wot's going through her head any more.

'Right were gonna go get this out, then you gotta give it back to Kriss.' I don't know how to play this for the best. If she gives it back he might just handle her different, I just don't know, all I can do is try.

We get to the shop and go in. The man's shocked. 'You back so soon?'

I walk over to the counter and pass the guy the paper.

'Oh, you want to take it out now?'

I look at Claire. The worst thing is I'm using Kriss's credit card, but the way I see it is at least he'll have it back, honestly though I don't know where they go from here. The man gets his money and he hands me the jewellery. I feel so much better.

'So wot now Jen?'

I take a deep breath. 'Come on, let's go home.' I can see she's scared but that's her business. There's some things you as a person do in your life that only you can sort out, and this is one of them. You can show someone the way but you can't walk it for them.

She knows she's fucked up. 'Will you talk to him for me?' she asks. I just nod. Where did it all go wrong? She's been slipping for a while now.

We get to the house and go in. My heart's going hard cos I know he's had it with her. I put the kettle on and go and wake Kriss up. I kiss him until he stirs. I love him so much I'm hoping he's not gonna be vex with me.

'Ello darling' he says, cuddling up to me.

'Baby I've got something for you.'

He rubs his eyes. 'Wot's that babe?'

I tell him to hold out his hand. He's looking at me like I'm nuts, but does it anyway. I hand him the jewellery. I see by the look on his face, it's priceless.

'How babe?'

I tell him wot happened.

'Wot, she's here?' I nod. With that he jumps out of bed and leaves the room. Then I hear him.

'I told you don't come back here! You need to get your things and leave.'

I have to stay out of it. He lets her know she will still get her money every month, after all that's still his sister, but if she can do something so low she can't be here any more, there's no trust. It was well sad. She was crying, saying she was sorry, but he weren't having none of it. There's only so much a person can take, family or not. I just sit there not knowing wot to do (well wot could I do or say? Nuffin.)

It made me feel so uncomfortable hearing a whole heap of things. I'm fucking shocked, I didn't think she was like that. They say you never know your friends fully, but shit this is a joke. I have to look at her with different eyes, ask myself if I ever really knew her.

Claire packs a few things and heads for the door. Kriss is in his room. My head's down cos I can't believe wot's happened. All this time Kriss has been covering up for her, now it's all out in the open, nowhere to hide.

'Jen' she says. I look at her, not knowing wot to say.

'Look after him' she's sobbing her heart out. 'Tell him I'm sorry.'

With that she turns round and leaves, just like that. I hear the door close. I don't know wot to do for the best, go in and see if he's OK or leave him alone. I'm upset as well, she's been my mate from time, if it weren't for her I wouldn't even know Kriss. I can't let him turn his back on her (that's his sister no matter wot). Not saying it's gonna be easy or nuffin, but family is family.

Kriss walks out of the room like nuffin, not even mentioning Claire. I think to myself, just leave it a day or so see how the land lies and take it from there. Maybe I should have stopped her from leaving.

But I don't really know wot's gone on. Kriss wouldn't go on like that for nothing. Trust, everything is nuffin when you're not around those you love.

He comes and sits with me, paperwork in hand, he treats everyone like business. I suppose that how he copes, I told you that's his thing (keeps people at arm's length). Even though the world is full of people it's a very lonely place to be at times. Claire should think herself lucky that he's still catering for her. She will have to prove herself before he can look at her again.

The paperwork is straightforward now Kriss has gone though it, yes it's all mine, no strings attached, just like that. He gets me to sign them cos they have to go back to finalize everything.

'Once everything is sorted Jen, we'll pop down, you can meet the staff and get the ball rollin darling.'

I kiss him.

'Wot's that for?' he says, smiling.

'For being you babe. Thank you for loving me. I won't let you down.'

He looks at me. 'You could never let me down, it's yours not mine. I'll help you as much as I can.'

With that his phone rings. I can see whoever it is, he ain't happy. It's Jay, his little brother Jamie has been hurt on the road. With that Kriss and I jump in the car and head down the hospital. When we get there Jay's pissed off big time. Jamie has been stabbed in the leg. He's only 15 and by all accounts he's in a bad way. Their mum Cindy is all over Jay.

'If it weren't for you doing wot you're doing your brother wouldn't be here' she's sayin. But you know wot it's like, this kids of today are hurry, come up they want it all now, that's the way it is.

Jay switches on her. 'It's all good when you're taking the money though init, that's all you ever care bout, you make me sick, move from me!'

Their mum likes a drink and goes though men like no one's business. When we were growing up Jay had it hard. His mum had one guy that she moved in when she had only just met him. He used to bruck (that's beat) up Jay, even I lost track of the amount of black eyes that boy had. He don't live at home any more, he can't even have Jamie there cos social services won't allow it. Jay's done a bit of stir for GBH and threats to kill. If the guy weren't Jamie's dad I feel say he would have done it. Thankfully Jay was only 15 at the time, but he gave the guy a right good kicking and in the end when everything came out Jay got like 18 months. Jamie's coming up for 16, then he can move out and be with his bruv.

Not every stabbing, shooting or killing is because of drugs or gangs, sometimes shit just happens. Jamie will let us know.

Kriss takes Jay outside for a bit of a breather. Cindy's been hitting the bottle hard, she stinks of drink. If it weren't for Jay, Jamie would have nuffin. He stays with him more time cos their mum is useless. I walk to the doors, I can see them (it's a bit heated).

I can hear Kriss. 'Kool down bruv, we'll sort it.' If it ain't one thing it's another. To tell the truth I don't know how much longer I can take all this. Before me an Kriss got together I saw everything the way it was, for wot it was. Cos I was out of the loop now I'm inner it come in like its madness every day. This ain't how I wanted it to be. When it's one of your own you can't help but take the law into your own hands and sort things out. Kriss won't do nuffin until he knows wot went down, and that's wot I love about him, he sees the whole picture. Too many youts are losing their lives over stupidity. It's like they wanna play bad man.

The police are here

Doing wot they do best, nothing. No one's saying nuffin (that's the code outta road). The feds are having a word with the hospital staff, then they make their way over to Cindy. She ain't no good, she's fucking pissed.

I text Kriss, *The police are here come now.* They make their way in, Jay's swearing. Kriss grabs him by the arm, 'Shut up man!'

So now the police are taking some details of who is who. Then they turn to Kriss.

'What's your name?' Kriss just looks at them. 'Why do you need to know who I am, that's not important?' The policeman carries on to say they're trying to build a picture of what happened.

'Well I weren't there so I can't help you, can I. Come on man, do your job.'

Everyone's pissed off, feelings are running high. Kriss has known Jamie all his life. I hate the smell of hospital so I go outside and smoke a fag.

Jamie's 15 and such a pretty boy, he gets all the girls, he can take his pick. 15 is a very funny age, on your way to be a grown up but not quite there yet you know? We all knew he was seeing some chick off ends and she's a bit older than him. I'm just hoping it had nuffin to do with her.

I stay outside awhile, its bloody cold. It's made me think about

184

Arron. He must have been so scared, an that was meant to be someone who loved him. Look wot happened there! It's his funeral at the weekend.

Now it's a waiting game, it's been hours. My mum always says no news is good news. I look over to see the time, 1.37 am. Kriss asks if I want to go and sit in the car. The smell and them little plastic chairs are a bloody nightmare, and Cindy ain't helping, she's got a bottle of gin in her bag an every now and then she takes a swig. She looks like she ain't washed for a year. Her hair's like one big massive lock all stuck together. There's food all down the front of her clothes, she's a fucking state. She don't deserve no kids, always putting drink an men first. That's why Jay has no dealing with her, he's just about for his brother. Back in the day Jay used to give his mum money to help with Jamie, until one day he went round there was no food in the house, not a slice of bread, nuffin, Jamie hadn't eaten for days. So now Jay buys the food over the net and it gets delivered to the house, an she's sayin that she wants nuffin to do with him she's got time.

The doctor's here. He's trying to get Cindy to understand wot's happened, but she's all shaking and shit. Since we've been here she's drunk about a litre of gin, swear down, no lie! She's all wobbling an dry-mouthed. Jay takes over the conversation, Kriss is with him, I can see them. Jay breaks down (it looks bad). Kriss is holding him, oh shit, thinking to myself, I'm getting a bit worried, Kriss looks over and gives me the nod, the relief I'm feeling wow he's all right well I hope so!

They shake hands with the doctor and Kriss calls me over, puts his arms round me an holds me tight. It seems like ages until he lets me go, then explains wot just happened. Jamie was stabbed in the leg but the knife hit the main artery, it took them a while to stop the bleeding, he's lost a lot of blood. The man that found him saved his life by using his tie, otherwise he's be dead now.

Tears roll down my face, I'm in shock. 'He's only a little boy, who would do this to him?' Kriss comforts me. 'Don't babe, he's all right.' But is he really, and where does this leave the rest of us? Jay won't leave the hospital without seeing Jamie.

Kriss asks if I want him to drop me home. 'Yer babe.' I know he ain't gonna stay with me, he has to be there for Jay and I understand that.

When we get there he makes me a cuppa. 'Babe, I've gotta go.' If anyone can get the low-down it will be Kriss. I sit and roll a spliff, trust me I need it. I must have crashed out, everything's catching up with me.

On the sofa

I wake up to sirens, police flying everywhere. My heart is beating so hard an fast I can hear it, I'm scared, my hands are clammy.

I pick up my phone to call Kriss, maybe that's the wrong thing to do. I put it back down. I find myself pacing up an down, checking the window, a minute feels like an hour. I sit down, just to get up again, have another look out the window, where is he? It's 5.30 am. I make a cup of tea, an with that I hear the door. I turn round.

'Babe' he looks drained. 'Jamie took a turn for the worse.'

I don't wanna hear this. I can't stop crying, he holds me close. 'Babe, he's stable now, Jay's with him.'

He goes and jumps in the shower. I don't know wot to do with myself, it's like I'm in a bad dream an can't find my way. He's in there a while. I curl up on the sofa and shut my eyes, just for a minute.

The next thing I know Kriss is carrying me to bed. I hear him say 'shhhhh babe it's me, you fell asleep'. I hold him tight, I love him so much words can't describe, I remember him kissing me. Nuffin happened, he's not like that!

We get woken up a few hours later. Jay's on the phone sayin Jamie's awake. Kriss don't hesitate, he's up and out the door, well not as cold-hearted as its sounds but in a life like ours that's how it feels sometimes. I read too much into things but that's just me.

I lie back down and drift off, it's been a long night (hoping Jamie is all right).

I get up at 9.36, no Kriss. Just lying there for a good 20 mins ceiling watching. I grab my phone an see a missed call from Naz, I check the time, it was sent 8.10 am. I phone him cos that's a bit strange, still, mans, them don't move like that for nuffin.

'Wot's good fam, wot's up?' I ask.

'Blood, I need to see you fam, ASAP.'

'Why, wot's going on bruv?' The phone went a bit funny. 'Jen, just come check me yer? Today.'

Shit, wot's that all about? I stay in bed tryin to think wot it could be. Fuck it, I jump in the shower and head over there.

On way to check Naz

So I get to the house, he's like all prang an ting. 'Wot's going on G?' I ask. He's looking kinda shook still. 'Wot man?'

He takes me through to the kitchen and that's it. 'Jen, wot happened to Jamie? I know who it was.' I look at him an ask 'Do I know him?' He's shakin his head. 'Na he comes an buys a draw off me now an then.'

'Who? Wot's his name?' He's tellin me the yout ain't from ends, he's from east. He's got an older sister that lives around here an his name's Soli. He was there earlier bragging about stabbing up some yout, cos he tried it on with Jamie's girl and she told him to fuck off and he weren't having it. But thinking about it I never see no girl at the hospital.'

I send Kriss a text, *Got some news holla.* My phone rings, it's Kriss. I tell him wot I know an hand the phone to Naz. They have words an make a meet. Naz hands the phone back.

'Babe you'll see me soon all right darling?' he says.

'OK bye babe' I reply and hang up. 'Naz I'm off bruv, nice one though, I'll see yer.' He walks me out. 'Jen, we kool though, yer?'

We've known each other a little while still, but he did piss me off with that Claire ting. But so is life.

I head over to see my mum. I try and distance myself, cos the way

189

things are right now, fuck knows wot's gonna go down. Kriss ain't the type of person to rush into nothing, he'll get all the info first and work on it, mould it to how he wants things to pan out. He's got such a good head on his shoulders he could go all the way, wotever he put his hands to.

I knock the door, mum looks pleased to see me. 'Hello darling' she says, kissing me an giving me a hug, one of them cuddles only a mother could give. Inside mum makes me some scrambled eggs on toast and tea. I'm like an old woman with my tea.

'Have you spoken to Kriss yet?' she asks.

I drink a bit of tea. 'Yer, it's all sorted, you were right mum.'

She lights a fag. 'What happened then, what did he say?'

'It is mine, he wants me to run up some menus for another place.'

Mum's looking at me. 'Oh my gosh' she says. 'I know I'm just gonna go with it and see where it takes me. Me and your dad's here if you need help.'

Bless her, I know how much they care about my welfare, well all of us. They have only ever shown us love and done the best they could for us. One day I'll make them proud. Mum says she's proud of us already, but there's so much I wanna do for them, holidays, a nice house, a comfortable life, they so deserve it. And that's in my reach, thanks to Kriss! I owe him so much.

Mum turns the telly on, it's one of them programmes where they buy things and sell them off for a profit. Some woman on there bought something for 40p and it sold for £1500. Them tings never happen to me.

Me an mum are having a right laugh, there's a couple outside. The woman is hitting wot looks like it could be her man, her mouth is like a toilet, dirty! She's bringing him out, telling everyone their business. I don't like them things. It's funny when you see it though. But me myself, I'm very private I don't like people knowing shit about me.

My mum's egging the woman on. 'Hit him, go on!' She's fucking naughty.

I can hear my dad snoring like its World War 3, everything just seems normal the way it should be, I'm glad for that. Abbie an Lucie are next door, they got a little girl named Izzy, she's 8 yrs old, sweet well mannered, you know the type.

My mum's showing me some email, she's trying to get the law changed on joint enterprise, it's not a good look, I've learnt so much.

The police say a group of people is a gang. How many people in a group does it take to form a gang? Just because you're with a group of friends, if one does summit you all get charged. It doesn't matter even if you knew nuffin about it! How is that right, one person can't know wot the other is thinking, how could they? (The law is a joke).

The stories out there can't all be wrong, there has to be some truth in wot's being said. The police are the biggest gang out there and yer we need help, cos with them in charge we don't have a hope in hell. They're the only gang allowed to carry guns by law, wot a joke. So from that we're all fucked (corrupt! That's wot they are).

So my mum is running off some cases to me, and to tell you the truth something needs to be done, there's so many youts out there in jail doing time for things they haven't done. It's really sad and the feedback from the people outta road, the response is amazing, my mum couldn't ask for more.

In the end we had to turn the computer off, it got a bit deep. I mean something like that affects the whole family. Most family units break down, nowhere to turn, no help. The law only tells you what they want you to hear, even when they fuck up. It's not their fault, so who then? Of course its them, they do wot they do cos they can.

That's wot my mum's on, she just wants the truth out there, and for things to change for the better, bless her she's doing her ting.

And then there's me, I'm trying to fly straight. Now I've got the means, a bit of hard work. I've got it all, but then there's Kriss. I try not to think about it too hard cos it would drive me nuts like now I don't know wah gawn, where he is, I understand cos trust me if it was one of mine all hell would break loose, you see me?

That's the problem, we don't have no trust in the feds so we would rather go sort it ourselves, but now mans them are just killing each other like it's nuffin, and the worst thing about it is people are losing their lives over shit, a wrong look there, chatting up a gal who's got a man, it's all fucked up. Wot are we doing to each other? It's one big mess.

I went home back to Kriss's having had a wicked time at home with mum, still no word from him, it's the quiet that's getting to me the most. I won't call him cos you just don't do them things you know? But the way he's left me hanging it's not fair.

I go and jump in the bath then head to bed, not knowing wot's going on. I was just there in bed, my brain working overtime, tick tock, can't sleep just there by myself, whole heap of stuff running through my mind.

I dozed off at some stage. I didn't sleep for long, still on my own. I got up and walked through to make a cuppa an there he was on the sofa sleeping like nuffin. I carried on making my tea, thinking is he taking the piss? There's me all worried not knowing wot's happening and then he just come in like that!

Then I hear 'babe?' I go to the door and just look at him, so he can see I ain't best pleased.

'Na babe, sorry, come.' I finish making my drink and go and sit with him. He lets me know Jamie's gonna be all right. I was happy for that bit of news. Then I asked him about the yout.

'Jen it's sorted, don't worry.' Just like that.

'Wot do you mean, wot have you done?'

'There's things you don't need to know and this is one.' He said it like I was no one. I looked at him, not really knowing who he was.

Got up and went back to the bedroom. I could hear him, 'babe come'. I weren't going, I can't believe he just said that.

This is the man I want to spend the rest of my life with and he's keeping things from me, wot kind of start is that? He came in trying to get round me, kissing, touchy feely.

'Stop it.' I just wasn't feeling it. 'If you don't trust me wot's the point?'

He never said anything for a minute, I couldn't believe it. Nuffin, then he said 'I love you Jen, that's all you need to know. I'll do anything for ya.'

I understand where he's coming from but I can't have us hiding things from each other, wotever it is then it's up to me to stay or go.

'Jen, you need to understand you're not always gonna know everything, some things it's best you don't.'

'Yer but that's up to me, I know you.' I said. He's shaking his head. 'That's the person you make me wanna be, that's the truth.' He's crying, I don't know wot to do. If I hold him then he's gonna think all this is forgotten, and if I don't how can I not?

I put my arms round him and just hold him, there's nothing he could tell me that would make me stop loving him, and that's my choice. We all have to make choices. Sometimes we make the wrong ones, but we learn from them.

Kriss did end up leaving the firm. Well I say leaving, he'll never let go, they've been there a long time but he's not involved like he was. To this day I worry he'll go back, it's in his blood, they were his family. But now it's all about us. Yes, we got married, it was a beautiful day, we've just got closer. He's my life.

The love nest is one of the best things ever. Leona and Maggie work for us now and they're together, wot a turnout! They're so happy, it's nice (bless).

Sonia and Shelly have gone travelling. We talk often. They're kool though, having a wicked time.

As for me, I've never been happier.

www.ingramcontent.com/pod-product-compliance
Lightning Source LLC
Chambersburg PA
CBHW060935180626
46817CB00004B/1552